JOURNEY TO SAN JACINTO

BOOK TWO

JOURNEY TO SAN JACINTO

Melodie A. Cuate

Texas Tech University Press

This book is typeset in MrsEaves. The paper used in this book meets the minimum
requirements of ANSI/NISO Z39.48-1992 (R1997).

Illustrations by Lindsay Starr

Library of Congress Cataloging-in-Publication Data
Cuate, Melodie A.

Journey to San Jacinto / Melodie A. Cuate.

p. cm. — (Mr. Barrington's mysterious trunk ; bk. 2)

Summary: When Mr. Barrington goes missing, his magic trunk transports
Hannah, Jackie, and Nick back to the Texas Revolution, where the girls carry
ammunition for General Houston and Nick becomes a soldier when the
Mexican army finds him hiding in a tree.

ISBN-13: 978-0-89672-602-4 (lithocase : alk. paper)

ISBN-10: 0-89672-602-9 (lithocase : alk. paper)

1. Texas—History—Revolution, 1835-1836—Juvenile fiction. [1.
Texas—History—Revolution, 1835-1836—Fiction. 2. San Jacinto, Battle
of, Tex., 1836—Fiction. 3. Time travel—Fiction. 4. Schools—Fiction.]
I. Title.

PZ7.C8912Joc 2007

[Fic]—dc22   2006029847

Printed in the United States of America
07 08 09 10 11 12 13 14 15 / 9 8 7 6 5 4 3 2 1
T S

Texas Tech University Press   Box 41037
Lubbock, Texas 79409-1037 USA
800.832.4042   ttup@ttu.edu   www.ttup.ttu.edu

To the Mexican drummer boy

CONTENTS

᚜᚛

HISTORICAL CHARACTERS

⊰⊱

Arnold, Hendrick (?–1849): He was a spy for the Texians during the Battle of San Jacinto and served under Deaf Smith.

Castrillón, General Manuel (?–1836): He was a general under Santa Anna in the Mexican army. After the Battle of the Alamo, he placed several Texian prisoners of war under his protection, but Santa Anna had the prisoners immediately executed. Castrillón was killed during the Battle of San Jacinto and was buried near Buffalo Bayou on Lorenzo de Zavala's land.

Cruz, Antonio (?–?): He was a member of Captain Juan Seguín's company. Cruz left the Alamo with Seguín during the Mexican siege to gather reinforcements. He served during the Battle of San Jacinto.

Dick (?–?): He was a free African American who served as a drummer for the Texians during the Battle of San Jacinto.

Diego (?–?): There is historical evidence of a Mexican drummer boy who died during the Battle of San Jacinto. (Author's note: Since I couldn't find the boy's name in any of the records, I named him Diego.)

Herrera, Pedro (1806–?): He was a private in Captain Juan Seguín's company and served during the Battle of San Jacinto.

Houston, Sam (1793–1863): He was born in Virginia. In 1827, he became the governor of Tennessee. In 1832, he moved to Texas. Houston was the commanding general of the Texas forces during the Battle of San Jacinto. Under his leadership, Texas gained its independence from Mexico.

Santa Anna, Antonio Lopez de (1794–1876): He was the President of Mexico and the commander of the Mexican army during the Texas Revolution.

Seguín, Juan (1806–1890): He organized a company of Tejanos to support the Texas Revolution. Seguín left the Alamo as a messenger before the Battle of the Alamo and led his men during the Battle of San Jacinto. Seguín held a burial service for the fallen defenders of the Alamo.

Smith, Erastus "Deaf" (1787–1837): A childhood illness caused his hearing problem. Smith served as a spy during the Texas Revolution. Houston ordered Captain Smith to destroy Vince's Bridge just before the Battle of San Jacinto to prevent Mexican soldiers from escaping.

Tarín, Manuel (1811–?): He was a private in Captain Juan Seguín's company and was present at the San Jacinto battlegrounds. Because he was ill at the time, Tarín was unable to participate in the Battle of San Jacinto. He was a corporal by the time he left the army.

Wells, James (?–?): He joined Sherman's volunteer company in March of 1836. He drove a munitions wagon to the San Jacinto battleground. Wells was compensated for the loss of a horse during the battle.

L.M.D. Guillaume, "The Battle of San Jacinto."
Courtesy of the R.W. Norton Art Gallery, Shreveport, LA.

JOURNEY TO SAN JACINTO

TEXAS
1836

Battle of San Jacinto

San Felipe de Austin

Gonzales

Harrisburg

San Antonio de Béxar

New Washington

Victoria

Goliad

Nuevo Laredo

GULF OF MEXICO

Matamoros

MEXICO

N
W   E
S

Area of Detail

——— Sam Houston and the Texian Army

- - - - - Santa Anna and the Mexican Army

✕ San Jacinto Battle Site

→ Direction of Army Movements

Cartography by Matt Crawford

Will you find your courage
as danger lurks about?
Will you find your courage
if your heart is filled with doubt?
A plea for help
floats on the air.
Will you stand firm
or just despair?
When friends have flown,
and you're alone,
will you find your courage?

CHAPTER ONE

❧ ❧

The Agreement

"Take a deep breath, Hannah," Jackie said. "There's nothing like it in the entire universe."

"What do you mean?" Hannah gazed through a store window at the display of new sneakers.

Studying her own reflection in the glass, Jackie flattened out strands of black hair that had worked loose from her ponytail. "It's mall air, the scent of brand-new everything!" She swung a small bag at her side as they strolled past the storefronts.

Hannah bit her lip and stopped at a small display in the center of the hallway. "Cool jewelry. I haven't seen this stand before."

"Forget the jewelry," Jackie whispered. "Check out the lady selling it."

Hannah looked up as the woman smiled at her. The clerk wore a bright turquoise skirt that swept the floor. Her spiky black hair was streaked with gray. Silver and gold bracelets jingled over both of her wrists.

"Wow, your eyes are different colors!" Jackie bubbled. "One's green and one's blue."

"Twelve-year-old girls are always so observant," the woman remarked.

Jackie stepped closer. "How do you know my age?"

The woman ignored Jackie's question. "May I help you find something?" she asked Hannah in a quavering voice. The dark pupils in the woman's eyes seemed to grow larger, like a cat watching its prey.

Hannah leaned over the counter. Her shoulder-length brown hair fell toward her face. She touched a silver ring with a dolphin leaping across it. "Do you have something more unusual?"

The woman patted the top of Hannah's hand. Her long nails were sharp against Hannah's skin. "I may have just what you want," the woman replied. She reached under the counter and removed a small velvety box covered with dust. As she blew across the top of it, the dust floated down like flecks of silvery glitter. She opened the box and turned it toward Hannah. Inside was a wide silver band.

"I'm not sure," Hannah mumbled. Tiny rows of

arrows decorated both edges of the ring. Zigzag, spiral, and diamond shapes filled the space between the arrows. "Look, Jackie." Hannah removed the ring from the box. "These are the same symbols as the ones on Mr. Barrington's trunk."

Jackie's eyes widened. She plucked the ring from Hannah's fingers and placed it back in the box. "The one with the dolphin is much better," Jackie insisted.

"Oh, but this one is old, very old," the woman said. "In fact, it came from deep in Mexico. Try it on." She gave the ring back to Hannah.

Hannah slid the ring on her index finger. "A perfect fit!" she said.

"Like it was made for you, my dear." The woman placed the empty box under the counter.

"I don't think you should buy it," Jackie muttered. Her ponytail bounced as she shook her head from side to side.

"Don't worry," Hannah said as she paid the woman for the ring. "The way it looks—it's just a coincidence."

Jackie checked her watch as they walked away from the stand. "Aren't we supposed to meet your mom in the food court?"

"We have to find Nick first. He's looking for a new CD."

Jackie made a face. "Can we sit at a different table when we eat?"

"Maybe," Hannah giggled. "He hates being with us, especially at the mall. Someone might see him."

"Your brother's such a pain."

Hannah held up her hand to admire her new ring as they stepped into the entertainment store. "I was lucky to find this."

"Creepy is more like it." Jackie shuddered. "That woman selling the jewelry was dressed like a fortune teller."

The girls stopped on the opposite side of a counter from Nick. He skimmed over the songs on the back cover of a CD. "Whoa . . . what smells?" he asked.

Hannah's brown eyes narrowed. "Duh, it's cologne. We were at Bath and Body Works, sampling different scents."

Nick smirked. "It smells more like the spray the guy used on the termites last week."

"You're so immature," Jackie snapped.

"Nice one, Nick," Hannah grumbled. "Come on. It's time to meet Mom in the food court."

Nick's eyes followed someone's movement on the other side of the store. "Go without me. I'm not hungry."

"Not hungry?" Jackie asked. "That's a first."

"Did you hear that noise, Hannah?" Nick grabbed at something in the air. "It's like a little fly buzzing around my head."

Jackie put her hands on her hips. "We should have left *you* back in time when we had the chance."

Hannah silently agreed. Only two short weeks ago, Nick had helped her open Mr. Barrington's mysterious trunk in her seventh-grade history classroom. A funnel of hazy smoke spun out of the trunk, surrounding her, Nick, and Jackie. Instantly, they were sent back in time, back to the Texas Revolution. Gunfire and cannonballs whistling overhead had welcomed them to 1836. It had been a terrifying and eye-opening experience.

Nick flipped through several more CDs. "You'd be picking cotton and begging for table scraps if I hadn't rescued both of you during the Battle of the Alamo."

"Rescued?" Jackie squeaked. "That's not exactly how it happened."

"Get real," Hannah muttered. "We all worked together to get home."

"Point of view, Hannah." Nick slid out another CD. "Let's not forget the Mexican soldier who aimed his bayonet at me."

Hannah's face softened. She felt the small carved cross dangling around her neck. She would never forget James Bowie, or the other brave Alamo defenders of the past. "We really ate lunch with David Crockett and watched Travis draw the line in the sand with his sword."

There was a spark in Nick's blue eyes as he concentrated

again on something behind Hannah. "You know we can't tell anyone," he mumbled. "They'd never believe it."

"But I have my cross, and Mr. Barrington knows what happened," Hannah disagreed.

Nick leaned toward Hannah. "Your teacher hasn't mentioned our little field trip back in time for two weeks. And when he does, I'm giving you a little advice. Stay away from that messed-up trunk."

"The trunk isn't in the classroom anymore. It's almost like it disappeared." Hannah's voice lowered to a whisper. "Something strange is going on. I can feel it in my bones."

"My sister the psychic," Nick laughed. His smile faded as he stared at Hannah. "Is that what you want? Another rerun of history?"

Hannah looked away. She picked out a CD and pretended to study the cover. "Ah, I didn't say that."

Two teenage girls walked across the store and stopped at a poster display at the end of the aisle. The girls giggled as they exchanged glances with Nick. He smiled back at them.

"That's why he isn't hungry," Hannah whispered to Jackie.

"I've seen those two at school," Jackie whispered back. "That girl with the long hair likes your brother."

Hannah rolled her eyes. "What do they see in him?"

"Who knows, but if he starts talking to them, we'll never get the chance to ask him about Mr. B."

"I'll handle this." Hannah tapped impatiently on the counter. "Hello, Nick, over here. We need to discuss something."

Turning back toward his sister, Nick scratched his head. "Huh?"

"Pay attention," Jackie hissed. "We've been trying to catch Mr. B when he's alone, but he's never by himself, and he hasn't been in the classroom after school."

"Sounds like he's avoiding you," Nick said. "Who can blame him?"

Hannah hurried around to Nick's side of the counter. "You have to go with us. You know, present a united front. We have to find out more about that trunk."

"Not interested." Nick started to walk away. He hesitated. "Do you have a couple dollars, Hannah? I'm a little short."

Hannah followed Nick down the aisle with Jackie right behind her. "I have money to lend you," Hannah offered.

"Thanks." Nick grinned as he held out his hand.

"It'll cost you," Hannah said.

"Just one little favor," Jackie hinted.

Nick's smile turned to a frown. He stared down at the CD he was carrying. Quickly opening her purse, Hannah removed a five-dollar bill. She waved it at her brother.

"Go with us to talk to Mr. Barrington," she demanded.

"Tomorrow morning before school," Jackie added.

Nick groaned.

As she flashed the money at him again, Hannah asked, "Do you want the CD or not?"

Nick snatched the money from Hannah's hand. "If Mr. Barrington's not there tomorrow, you're on your own."

⊰⊱

CHAPTER TWO

The Substitute

Early Monday morning, Hannah hurried down the hall to Mr. Barrington's room. Jackie waited outside the open classroom door with a small mirror in her hand, checking her hair and applying some lip gloss. "Where's Nick?" she asked.

"He stopped by his locker. He'll be here in a few minutes," Hannah replied. She peeked into the classroom. A young woman stood beside Mr. Barrington's desk, shuffling through files. She slammed one file drawer closed and opened the next. Her bright red hair was pulled back and twisted into a bun with a pencil jammed through it. Loose frizzy strands hung down on her face. She wore gray plaid pants and a black hooded jacket, at least two sizes too large. Beneath her jacket was a white shirt with a man's striped tie. Settling down in the teacher's chair, she adjusted her plastic-framed glasses.

Hannah grimaced. "Not a substitute today."

"Look at her clothes," Jackie snickered. "Where does our principal get these people?"

The substitute, aware of her audience, turned toward the door. "Don't just stand out there and stare," she called out. "It's impolite. Maybe you can help me with my conundrum."

Both girls entered the room and approached the teacher's desk. "Sorry we spied on you," Hannah said. "I'm Hannah Taylor, and this is Jackie Montalvo."

"What's a conundrum?" Jackie asked. "A band instrument?"

"It's a difficult problem or puzzling situation," the woman explained. "Let me introduce myself. I'm Miss Barrington, your substitute teacher."

Hannah looked at Jackie. They muffled a giggle. "Are you related to Mr. Barrington?" Hannah asked.

Miss Barrington brightened. She removed her jacket and laid it over the back of her chair. "Why, of course. He's my uncle."

Somewhat disappointed, Hannah set her backpack down on a student's chair. "Why isn't Mr. Barrington here?"

Journey to San Jacinto

A stack of books covered one corner of the desk. As Miss Barrington extracted a manila folder from underneath them, the top two books fell to the floor with a thud. "My uncle is taking a few days off. He was supposed to meet me here this morning. His jeep is in the parking lot, but he hasn't shown up yet. That's half of my conundrum." Miss Barrington opened the folder and sorted through the papers inside. "There are no lesson plans anywhere. That's the other half."

Hannah picked up the books from the floor and placed them back on the desk. "Where's your uncle going?"

"He was extremely secretive about that," Miss Barrington said as she closed the folder.

"Your uncle definitely has lots of secrets," Jackie agreed.

As she leaned back in the chair, Miss Barrington studied the girls. "What secrets?"

Hannah took in a deep breath and let it out slowly. She turned the silver ring around and around her finger. "It's his trunk . . . and what's in it."

Miss Barrington pushed her glasses higher on her nose and headed toward a closet in the back of the classroom. She turned the doorknob and pulled, but the door opened only a few inches. Miss Barrington gripped the edge of the door and pulled harder. The door seemed to groan as she forced it wide open. "Is this it?"

Inside the closet was a dark brown antique trunk covered with a thick coat of dust and filmy spiderwebs. Discolored and torn labels stuck to the sides of the trunk told a story of where it had traveled: San Antonio, Guadalajara, Veracruz, Monclova, San Jacinto, Jalapa, and Zacatecas. Arrows, spirals, zigzags, and diamond-shaped markings were carved on the sides and top, racing around the trunk in faded shades of yellow, orange, blue, teal, and red.

Hannah and Jackie rushed to the back of the room. "So that's where Mr. B hid the trunk," Jackie said.

"And someone was here earlier." Hannah pointed to muddy footprints leading from the classroom door to the trunk. They became less noticeable as they entered the closet.

"We'll worry about that mud later." Miss Barrington patted the top of the trunk. "Give me a hand, Hannah."

Hannah grabbed a leather handle on one side of the trunk, and Miss Barrington tugged from the opposite end. Together, they dragged it out of the closet.

"That thing's really heavy!" Hannah exclaimed. As she brushed dust off her hands, Hannah noticed her ring; the symbols had started to glow. No one else had seen it. Hannah quickly removed the ring and slipped it into the front pocket of her jeans.

"My uncle does collect unique artifacts from the past."

Miss Barrington paced around the trunk. "I wonder what he has in there."

Hannah's eyes sparkled as she traced a capital H and an A in the dust covering the lid of the trunk. Suddenly, particles of dust shifted and an $N N A H$ appeared to the right of the first two letters. Catching her breath, Hannah rubbed her hand over her name, erasing it before Miss Barrington or Jackie could notice. "This trunk really attracts dust," Hannah mumbled nervously.

The latch of the trunk had a rusty padlock suspended from it. On the face of the lock was a square with a clover-shaped design in the center. Miss Barrington grasped the lock that guarded the secrets of the trunk and yanked at it.

"Stop!" Jackie shrieked. "You have no idea what'll happen once you pop the lid on that thing."

Miss Barrington chuckled. "A bit high-strung, aren't you?"

Jackie stomped across the room. She grabbed a handful of tissues from the teacher's desk and hurried back to the trunk. After dusting off a portion of the top, Jackie sat down on it. Her eyes opened wide as she leaned forward so far that her fingers clung to the edge of the trunk for balance. "It all starts out with these strange noises." Her words came fast and shaky. "Then a mini-tornado swooshes out of the trunk. Once it surrounds you, there's no turning back."

Miss Barrington's eyebrows flared up in surprise. "You're perfect for the drama club."

Jackie patted the top of the trunk. "This is real life-and-death stuff, Miss B. As long as I'm sitting here, no one opens it."

CHAPTER THREE

Hannah Opens the Trunk

"What's your take on this, Hannah?" Miss Barrington knelt down in front of the trunk. She smoothed out the wrinkles on a loose label of Mexico City.

"Things happened, all right." Hannah moved to the rear of the trunk, right behind Jackie. The dust stirred and rearranged itself, forming more letters, one at a time. Hannah held her breath as *H E L P* gradually appeared on the back of the trunk. Quickly grabbing the tissue from Jackie's hand, Hannah wiped the message away.

Jackie blurted out, "When Hannah's brother opened the tiny doors on this itty-bitty model of the Alamo we found in the trunk, smoke started swirling around.

Before we knew it, we were in front of the actual Alamo, and it was 1836."

"Sounds like you've seen too many movies," Miss Barrington said.

Jackie snapped her fingers in front of Miss Barrington. "*Poof!* Suddenly, we were back in time. Cannonballs were flying over us."

"David Crockett looked a lot like your uncle," Hannah said.

Miss Barrington smiled. "Crockett is actually an ancestor of ours."

"We almost got ourselves killed!" Jackie sputtered. "Are you listening to me?"

"Of course I am. Hmm . . . I saw some keys earlier." Miss Barrington hurried back to the teacher's desk. She shuffled a few things from side to side in the center drawer and picked up a ring filled with long rusty keys. "One of these must work." The heavy keys clinked together as she headed back to the trunk. "Here's one with a clover on the top. It matches the lock perfectly."

Jackie jumped to her feet. "Let's get out of here," she squeaked.

"You . . . you go," Hannah said. "Miss Barrington has no idea what's about to take place."

"Not without you," Jackie insisted stubbornly.

Miss Barrington fit the key into the lock. She pursed her lips and jiggled it. With a snap, the lock popped open.

Miss Barrington removed the lock and cracked open the lid on the trunk. Before she could lift it higher, Jackie slammed the lid back down.

"All I saw were books," Miss Barrington scolded. "There's nothing dangerous about books."

Hannah sat down on a chair. She ran her finger along the edge of the trunk. "The second time's the charm. That's when everything inside is different."

"Don't open it, Hannah!" Jackie begged.

"I have to show her." Hannah inched her chair closer to the trunk. There was something compelling about discovering who needed her help. Was it Mr. Barrington? The lid creaked as Hannah opened it. A puff of dust rose in the air.

Miss Barrington applauded as she gazed into the trunk. "You're an excellent magician, Hannah. What an exceptional assortment of relics!"

Everything inside the trunk was different. Jackie's mouth dropped open. "Uh-oh, here we go again."

The trunk held many clues to the past. On the left side, a riding whip rested on the top of dark-covered books that were stacked in an orderly manner. A neatly folded dark blue uniform lay on the opposite side. Gold trim ran around the edges of its red collar and cuffs, and gold buttons stood at attention down the front. Three medals hung from ribbons pinned to the left side. A pair of rusty spurs lay in the corner next to a few rolled-up papers.

Miss Barrington picked up a tarnished bugle. "Just imagine," she mused, "this instrument was probably played at some battle years ago. The song would indicate what position the men would take on the battlefield."

"Let's not imagine anything else," Jackie chimed in nervously. "Come on, Hannah. Let's leave."

Hannah shook her head. "I didn't hear any cymbal sounds. Remember, the cymbal sounds start before the room gets smoky."

"If anything else strange happens," Jackie sighed, "we're out of here."

Miss Barrington laid the bugle on her lap and peered back into the trunk. She chose a black leather-bound book to page through. "There's a date inside, 1836. It mentions the Brazos River and planting corn. This must have belonged to a Texan."

"They sometimes called themselves Texians in the early 1800s," Hannah explained.

"Texian? That's a quaint term," Miss Barrington said.

Drawn to the trunk, Hannah reached in. "These are huge!" She pulled out a pair of tan gloves and tried them on. The buttery-soft leather reached up past her elbows.

"Those are gauntlets," Miss Barrington said. "They must have belonged to a large man."

Jackie stooped over the trunk. She eased out a piece of paper from beneath some journals. The deteriorating edges were wrinkled and yellow. "Look at this," she muttered. "It's a song, 'Will You Come to the Bower?' What's a bower, Miss B?"

"It's a pretty place in a garden where you would find flowers and vines crawling around a trellis," Miss Barrington said. "I think it's a song a small group of musicians played during the Battle of San Jacinto. Imagine warriors striding onto the battlefield while music is playing." She puffed at a strand of red hair hanging over her face and lifted up a long delicate chain from the trunk. A gold pocket watch swung from the end of the chain. "Oh my, this is a rare piece! I can barely make out the initials engraved on the front."

"The Battle of San Jacinto," Jackie and Hannah whispered in unison. A lonely bugle call echoed in the distance. Hannah felt a chill on the back of her neck.

Ignoring what Miss Barrington had found, Jackie tugged on Hannah's sleeve. "Let's go!" Jackie urged.

It was too late. The bugle sound grew louder. A stream of ash-colored smoke snaked its way out of the trunk. The smoke formed a swirling funnel, small at first and then gradually larger, twisting and turning around them. Hannah's feet felt like they were cemented to the floor. Everything started moving in slow motion.

"W-h-a-t's h-a-p-p-e-n-i-n-g?" Miss Barrington shouted over the tumult. Her voice warped and stretched like a music box winding down.

"I w-a-r-n-e-d y-o-u!" Jackie screamed. She placed

her hands over her ears to deaden the sound.

Nick entered the classroom. A misty film had wrapped around Hannah, Jackie, and Miss Barrington. Scowling at his sister, Nick dropped his backpack to the floor. "I told you not to do this!" he shouted.

Hannah could barely hear Nick over the thunderous noise. He staggered forward as the clamor grew even louder. The closer Nick got, the slower he moved. The floor began to roll up and down, resembling the surface of an ocean. It was almost like he was walking over one of those trick mirrors at the carnival, the kind with a wavy reflection.

"N-i-c-k!" Hannah cried. The smoke completely covered Hannah, and in that instant, everything went dark.

CHAPTER FOUR

James Wells

Hannah was sitting on the ground in the center of a meadow. She gazed down at her clothes. She wore a long blue dress with a lacy white collar. Her shoes had transformed into low button-up boots. A trace of a smile appeared. "We're here," she said softly.

Nearby, Jackie's and Miss Barrington's heads popped up over the tall grass. As Hannah straightened her hair, she caught a glint of silver. It was her ring. *How did this get back on my finger?* Hannah wondered.

Several jays squawked in angry spurts. They soared overhead, flying into the thick pine trees bordering the meadow. The gray sky was filled with billowing thunder-clouds, containing the rain for the moment.

"Where are we?" Miss Barrington murmured. She rose up on wobbly legs.

"Following your uncle into the past," Hannah explained as she stood up. She pulled Jackie to her feet.

"Thanks," Jackie mumbled. She bent over and straightened out her long dress. A delicate pattern of orange and brown flowers covered the pale yellow fabric. "Yellow is *so* not my color."

"Hannah," Miss Barrington said, "what makes you think Uncle David is here? There's no one in sight."

"Oh, there are plenty of clues," Hannah replied.

"They're all tied up with what's in that spooky trunk of his," Jackie added.

"Clues like the song 'Will You Come to the Bower'?" Miss Barrington asked.

"That's right," Jackie said. "Plus, you mentioned Mr. B was missing. He's here all right."

"Even your glasses match the time period we're in, Miss Barrington," Hannah reflected.

Stunned by everything unfamiliar, Miss Barrington removed the gold wire-rimmed glasses and examined them. "Where did these come from?" Then she touched the green calico fabric of her dress. Her long sleeves puffed out from the shoulders and narrowed down at the cuffs. "We are back in time. How utterly exciting!"

Lifting up her skirt a few inches, Jackie glared at her

petticoats. Layers of ruffles trimmed the edges of the undergarments. "We'll see how excited you are after dodging a few cannonballs." She pouted as she brushed dirt off the endless amount of fabric. "I hate these clothes. The sooner we find Mr. B, the sooner I get my comfy jeans back."

"Nick!" Hannah called out. "Where's Nick?"

"He was right in front of us," Jackie mumbled. She shook a few blades of grass out of her ponytail. "And he was really mad at you for opening that trunk."

"Perhaps he was left behind," Miss Barrington suggested as she slid her old-fashioned glasses back on. She squinted as she tried to focus.

Hannah spun slowly around. All she could see were grassy land and trees—no buildings or people, and definitely no Nick. The silence of the outdoors seemed to have swallowed them up.

"If Nick's here," Jackie remarked, "he's not gonna be a happy camper."

Hannah cringed. "Maybe he'll get over it by the time we find him."

"He'll never let you forget this one, Hannah," Jackie said.

But Mr. Barrington needs our help! Hannah thought. *Nick will have to understand.*

Suddenly, they heard a horse's whinny, followed by the

snapping of a whip. "Tarnation," a man hollered in a gruff voice.

The heads of two black horses emerged from the line of pine trees. A short man trudged around to the front of the animals. His pant legs were stuffed into mud-splattered boots, and he had on a tan leather vest over a dirty white shirt. A pistol stuck out from the side of his wide belt. He tugged on the halter of one of the horses. "Come on, Jenny! You and Sadie can do it!"

After considerable effort on the part of the horses and the man, a second pair of horses and a covered wagon appeared. The man put an arm around the closest horse. "I knew ya wouldn't let me down," he crooned. "Let's git goin', girls." The man climbed up into the wagon and cracked his whip. As the wagon eased into the clearing, he shouted, "How-dy-doo, gals! Why y'all here by yer lonesome? Have yer menfolk all gone a-huntin'?"

Jackie shuddered. "He looks like he needs a bath," she whispered.

"He hugs horses," Hannah whispered back. "He must be a nice guy, even if he is a little dirty."

Miss Barrington pushed her hair behind her ears. Red waves rippled past her shoulders. She smiled, but there was a cautious look in her eyes. "We're here by ourselves," she said.

The man chuckled as he brought the wagon to a halt.

"Where are my manners?" He politely removed a hat with a wide floppy brim and combed his fingers through his tangled, greasy hair. "I'm James Wells," he announced as if he were the president of the United States. "Jest call me James."

Miss Barrington took a small step forward. "I'm Georgia Barrington, and this is Hannah and Jackie."

James raised an eyebrow. "Barrington, ya say? Met a man by the name of Barrington a day or so ago. Strangest thing, he come out of them trees without nothin', no food, no water, no weapons."

"What did he look like?" Hannah asked.

"Taller than me with dark hair," James replied. "Don't rightly remember more."

"That's Mr. B," Jackie declared. "Where did he go?"

"Took off with some fellers. They was all fixin' to join up with Houston." James scratched at the whiskers on his unshaven chin. "I bet the three of you skedaddled out of town when Mexican soldiers marched in. Well, yer not safe here, not with the revolution goin' on. That's fer dern sure." His loud voice rang through the meadow.

Miss Barrington walked along the length of the wagon. She glanced up into the canvas-covered interior. "May we ride with you?"

"Reckon so. I'm headin' southeast," James said before he spat to the side.

"Eew," Jackie gasped as she took a step back. "Maybe we should go north."

James winked at Jackie. "When my wagon got bogged down in the mud from all this intolerable rain we've been havin', I got behind the others. I'm trailin' the army, although these horses of mine are a mite stubborn. The wagon's plumb full of ammunition and supplies I'm totin' fer General Houston. Y'all have to take turns ridin' and walkin'."

"Houston," Hannah repeated to herself. Mr. Barrington would be interested in finding General Houston. "Let's go with James," Hannah agreed.

"You first," Jackie whispered. She nudged Miss Barrington toward the wagon. "He smells bad."

"After you walk a few miles," Miss Barrington said, "you'll be anxious for your turn to ride." Miss Barrington climbed up into the wagon and sat next to James. He smiled broadly, revealing a missing tooth.

James grabbed the reins. "Giddy up, girls!" he bellowed. "Don't embarrass me in front of these purty gals!" After a few neighed complaints and snorts from the horses, the wagon wheels began to roll. James whistled "Yankee Doodle" while Hannah struggled with her long dress as she waded through the knee-high prairie grass. Even though she was worried about her brother and teacher, she was excited to be on another adventure.

The songs James whistled helped the time pass by faster. He knew a variety of folk songs and hymns. Soon Miss Barrington's light soprano voice added words to the music. "Amazing grace! How sweet the sound . . ."

Once they finished the last verse, James brought the horses to a stop. "Who's ridin' next?"

Hannah chewed on a fingernail. *I do have a few questions to ask him,* she thought. Her mind made up, she traded places with Miss Barrington.

"We're kind of lost," Hannah said as the wagon lurched forward. "Where exactly are we, James?"

"Almost to Harrisburg. Ya know where that is?"

"Near San Antonio?"

"Nope, it's on the east side of Texas. The next town beyond Harrisburg is New Washington. They're almost within shoutin' distance of each other. New Washington sits smack dab on the Gulf Coast."

Hannah clutched her seat as she bounced from side to side from the bumpy ride. "How long before we catch up with General Houston?"

"I don't rightly know, missy," James replied. "It might be days. Look up at those dark thunderheads rollin' this way. We're in fer a gulley washer."

"A what?"

"Ya don't know what a gulley washer is?"

Hannah shook her head.

"It's a hard rain that washes away everythin' in its path."

Hannah frowned as she studied the clouds. She hadn't forgotten the message that had mysteriously appeared in the dust on the trunk. A gulley washer would slow them down.

Before long, it was Jackie's turn to ride in the wagon. Hannah walked beside Miss Barrington, noticing the signs of spring that dotted the land. Hannah paused to pick wildflowers until she carried a complete bouquet of vibrant spring colors.

Suddenly the wagon jerked as James pulled up hard on the reins. The horses slowed almost to a stop. In one fast motion, James pulled a rifle and a powder horn out from under the seat; then he placed the reins in Jackie's hands. He slung the leather strap tied to the powder horn over one shoulder. "Hey, what do I do with these things?" Jackie asked.

James jumped from the wagon and bolted toward a grove of oak trees. Hannah stared into the wooded area for signs of wild animals or Mexican soldiers.

BANG! The sound of the rifle cut through the air. James slipped his arm into the sling attached to his rifle, pulled a pistol from his belt, and sprang into the thicket.

Jackie set the reins down on the seat and stood up to get a better view. "What's going on?" she yelled.

BANG! Gunfire rang out again. The horses, spooked

by the noise, stirred and whinnied. With nothing to hold them back, they took off like racers at the Kentucky Derby.

"Help!" Jackie shrieked. Frightened even more by the girl's scream, the horses picked up speed. Jackie's arms flailed in the air as she toppled backwards into the wagon.

The four wild-eyed horses and their wagon sped toward the trees, followed by Hannah and Miss Barrington. "We'll save you!" Hannah shouted. As she ran, the hem of her dress twisted in the long grass and wrapped itself around her ankles. Hannah screamed as she tumbled to the ground. The flowers she carried flew from her hands in a colorful explosion.

"Stop the horses, James!" Miss Barrington shouted.

"What in tarnation is goin' on?" James roared. He plodded through the brush, dragging a dead hog by one of its hind legs. When he saw the runaway wagon, he leaned his rifle against a tree and dropped the hog. Even though the horses had slowed, they still trotted in his direction.

James gave one long shrill whistle and jogged to the wagon. "Whoa, girls," he said, grabbing the front horse by its halter. He led them away from the trees to a grassy spot, then set the brakes and unhooked a rope hanging on the outside of the wagon.

"Would y'all take a looky at what I kilt!" James strutted back to the dead hog. The animal was black with white spots. He proudly lifted its head up by a sharp tusk. "We'll have some good eatin' tonight."

Hannah put a hand over her mouth. *It has fangs,* she thought.

By the time Hannah and Miss Barrington reached the wagon, James had already tied the rope around the hog's snout and thrown the other end over the nearest tree branch. Wrapping the rope around his hands, he tugged until the dead animal swung beneath the tree. Blood dripped from its open mouth. Once the loose end of the rope was tied securely to the tree, James pulled out a bowie knife from a sheath on his belt. "Who's gonna help me gut out this wild hog?"

Rubbing her head, Jackie peered over the edge of the wagon bed. "What does 'gut out a hog' mean?" she moaned.

Hannah bit her lip. "I think we're about to find out what that pig had for lunch."

"Eww, that's gross!" Jackie wrinkled her nose. She swung her leg over the side of the wagon and climbed down.

Miss Barrington put her arm around Jackie's shoulder. "We should be grateful we'll have a decent meal," Miss Barrington said.

"Someone ought to tell James that ham comes sliced from the deli," Jackie muttered.

Journey to San Jacinto

As they gathered around James, he slit the hog down the stomach. The innards spilled to the ground in a wet, gooey mass. He grinned at the shocked expressions on the girls' faces. "Y'all act like ya ain't never seen anythin' like this before. Surely ya seen yer pa split open a critter he's kilt."

Jackie covered her eyes with her hands and then peeked through them. "I can't eat that," she moaned.

James's eyes crinkled up at the sides as he chuckled at Jackie's reaction. Suddenly, his laughter stopped as he glared at something behind Jackie. As he stepped to the side, he reached out for his rifle.

"Uh-oh," Hannah mumbled.

Four well-armed men wearing large *sombreros* rode up on horseback. The last man led a packhorse. One rider carried a rifle across his lap; the other three had rifles inserted in scabbards attached to their saddles. All of the strangers had knives and pistols tucked into their belts. The dangerous men stared down at them.

Jackie scurried behind James and squeaked, "Are they on our side, James?"

"I don't know, child," he responded in a serious tone. "Better say a prayer, cuz by the looks of things, we're in one devil of a fix."

CHAPTER FIVE
⚜

Nick's Dilemma

Nick felt the rough ground against his face. A cool breeze tousled his hair as he turned his head to the side. Slowly opening his eyes, he spat out dirt and grass. His body ached and his head throbbed. The world spun like a merry-go-round. "What a wild ride," he mumbled.

He stood up stiffly and shook out the knots in his body. There was no one in sight, only endless prairie. Several gnarled trees were sprinkled across the country-side, while jackrabbits played tag between bushes.

"Hannah, you can come out now!" Nick shouted. The teasing wind picked up his voice and carried it away. There was no response.

Dusting off his pants, he realized his clothes were different. Instead of jeans and a T-shirt, he was wearing baggy pants and a soft long-sleeved shirt. Layered over the shirt was a brown wool jacket. Some of the buttons were missing on the front of the jacket, but it was warm enough to keep out the cold air beginning to gust toward him. His scuffed boots showed plenty of wear. At least they were comfortable.

A gray wide-brimmed hat lay on the ground. Nick picked it up and set it firmly on his head. Under the hat was a cloth bag that held a partial loaf of bread, a wedge of white cheese, and some jerky. "So much for take-out food of the past," he grumbled.

As he set the bag aside, Nick noticed another oddly shaped object, a dried gourd. Strips of leather bound a stopper to the top, and something swished inside when he shook it. He unwound the leather strips, pulled out the stopper, and smelled the contents. With a curious expression, he took a sip. "Man, what muddy river did this come out of?" he coughed.

Nick had to find his sister, and the ruts on the path would be his map. Twin grooves cut deeply into the earth, hinting that wagon wheels had created them. Civilization must be at both ends, but which way should he go? He inhaled deeply and went with a gut feeling.

As he hiked along the path for what seemed like hours, he snacked on the food and kept up a steady pace. After a while, he noticed an unusual puff of smoke floating skyward in the distance. It expanded, forming a mushrooming cloud. A green, white, and red flag arose from the cloud. As it flapped in the wind, Nick was able to make out an eagle in the center section. It was a Mexican flag! The smoke was a dust cloud created by marching soldiers and men on horseback.

This is definitely not a good sign, Nick thought. Off to his right was a small stand of trees, the perfect place to hide. He sprinted across a small field into the timber. Choosing a towering tree in the grove, he grabbed a lower limb, swung up into the branches, and climbed with ease toward a leafy area. Nick sat down on a large branch and leaned against the trunk to wait.

A soft drum cadence grew louder as the Mexican soldiers marched closer and closer. Men's voices called to one another in Spanish. Horses' hooves pounded the earth in an uncanny rhythm, coming nearer.

Nick remembered what the Mexican army had done to the Alamo defenders. There had been no survivors. What if they caught him?

Within minutes, soldiers crowded under the trees. Dropping their packs, they stood their muskets against each other in spiraling circles. The men reclined against the tree trunks or relaxed on the ground in the shade. Even though the air was cool, traces of sweat trickled down their faces.

Most of the soldiers wore white trousers and navy blue jackets with bright red collars and cuffs. Some had on tall dark hats while others wore shorter crowned hats with wide brims. As they rested, the men pulled out food from their packs for a quick meal. Everything about the Mexican army fascinated Nick, and yet he wished they would march away.

Nick felt around for the gourd containing his water. He removed the top and took a drink. As he set the container back on the branch, the gourd's rounded bottom wobbled unsteadily. Down it plummeted, spilling water as it landed right between a soldier's feet. Nick cringed. His presence was no longer a secret.

The startled soldiers looked from the gourd to Nick. Some pointed at him and laughed. Others jumped to their feet, rapidly affixing bayonets to their muskets. They spoke enthusiastically to one another.

Nick quickly climbed higher as five sharp bayonets poked and prodded in his direction. The soldiers seemed to be enjoying this game with Nick as the prized piñata.

The sound of a horse's snort brought the soldiers to attention. An officer on a sleek black stallion rode up and shouted at Nick, *"¡Bájate de allí!"* The feisty horse pawed the ground restlessly, sensing the rider's irritation. Immediately, the soldiers moved aside.

The officer's neatly trimmed mustache and beard was streaked with gray. He wore a dark blue jacket and white trousers, and his high red collar and cuffs were decorated with gold braid. Gold buttons completed the front of his uniform. He sported a magnificent navy-colored hat, adorned with red, white, and green plumage. A long shiny saber hung at his side.

"¡Bájate de allí!" the officer repeated loudly as he glared at Nick.

Even though Nick couldn't understand the words, he knew what the man wanted. First tossing his bag of food down, Nick lowered himself little by little to the ground. His mind raced, trying to figure out how to communicate with an angry Mexican officer.

"¿Qué haces aquí, muchacho?" snapped the man. Nick lifted the brim of his hat up a few inches and stared into the man's dark eyes. The officer urged his horse forward until he was practically on top of Nick. The spirited stallion snorted and stomped on the ground. Nick reached out, took hold of the horse's halter, and proceeded to pet the large brute on its neck.

A younger officer on horseback joined the first. They spoke to each other in Spanish. Then the older officer turned back to Nick. *"¿Qué haces aquí, muchacho?"* he thundered.

Nick jerked his hat off. "I don't know what you're saying." The only phrase Nick ever used in Spanish was *"Más salsa, por favor"* to top his enchiladas in a Mexican restaurant. He exhaled in frustration.

The two officers exchanged glances. The older one demanded in English, "Boy, who are you and where are the others? Speak quickly before I lose what is left of my temper."

Clutching his hat in his hands, Nick tried to remain calm. "I'm Nicholas Taylor, and there are no others."

"Nicholas," the older officer said in a slow, deliberate tone. "My name is General Manuel Castrillón. Are you certain you are alone? Perhaps you have some well-armed Texian friends up ahead, waiting for us. You are very young to be here by yourself, surrounded by His Excellency's finest *soldados.*"

The younger officer withdrew a sword from his scabbard and aimed it within an inch of Nick's throat. The sword glistened in the light of the setting sun. "I'm telling the truth," Nick gulped, trying not to move. "Why would I hide if I were leading you to an ambush?"

General Castrillón motioned for the younger officer to put his sword away. The black stallion pushed his muzzle into Nick's face, almost begging to be petted again. "I see my Cesar accepts you," General Castrillón remarked. "That is most unusual. My horse is trained to attack men who get too close."

Nick took a deep breath and held it for a moment. "I'm not afraid of horses. They can kind of tell when someone likes them." Nick rubbed Cesar's nose.

"You show much bravado, my young friend. We will

see if you are telling the truth. You will ride beside me until I can decide what to do with a young *norteamericano.*" The general waved his arm and called to someone. A soldier rode up, leading a scrawny brown mare by its reins. Its coat was scruffy, its eyes dull.

How could I ever escape on that old nag? Nick thought. The soldier held the reins toward Nick and grunted.

"I have a better idea," Nick suggested. "Why don't you just forget you saw me, and I'll be on my way?"

General Castrillón's expression was unreadable, his eyes unwavering. Nick's face grew warm with embarrassment. "If you insist on leaving," General Castrillón finally stated, "so be it. But before you go, take a good look at my men. They are extremely well-trained soldiers, and many of them despise *norteamericanos.*"

Nick felt his skin prickle. General Castrillón cleared his throat. "Now, take another long look, my young friend, at the very sharp tips on their bayonets. You will have to pass by many of them when you go on your way." He gave Nick a stern look. "I wish you luck, Nicholas. *Adios.*" The general backed up his horse and prepared to move on.

A lone bugle sounded. Nick watched hundreds of men falling into formation. The soldiers eyed him suspiciously as they walked by. Some had fierce expressions.

"Hold on!" Nick shouted. "Don't leave without me!"

He picked up his bag of food and rushed over to General Castrillón. The general nodded in agreement and before Nick could reconsider, he was sitting on an old brown horse beside a Mexican officer.

CHAPTER SIX

⚞ ⚟

The Perils of Jackie

"**B**uenas tardes," a man announced from the top of a tall palomino. A wide sombrero shadowed his face. Black wavy hair fell below his collar, and his beard was longer than James's. A colorful blanket with geometric designs hung loosely over his shoulders; underneath the blanket he wore a leather coat. Embossed leather leggings, tied just below the knees, covered the lower half of his pants and flared out over his boots. Holding a rifle in front of him, the man nudged his horse ahead of the other riders.

James protectively shooed Hannah behind him. "Do any of y'all know any Spanish?" he growled. "I only know enough words in that language to git me a cup of coffee."

"I do," Miss Barrington said eagerly, struggling to push her unruly hair out of her face. The north wind whipped it back again. "I'm fluent in Spanish and French. I also know a smattering of Italian, but . . ."

James stomped over to Miss Barrington. "Quit jawin' and talk to the feller!"

Completely ignoring James, Miss Barrington walked toward the strangers and smiled at the man on the palomino. She politely extended her arm and shook his hand. As she chatted with him in Spanish, the other men in the group relaxed, adding in a few words here and there. The strangers were cordial, but there was a seriousness about them.

Within a few minutes, Miss Barrington turned back to James and the girls. "These Tejanos are scouts for General Houston's army. They're ranchers and farmers by trade, but for now, they're soldiers."

"They look mighty suspicious to me," James hissed just above a whisper. He waved his hand, motioning for Hannah and Jackie to remain behind him.

"I can't see back here," Jackie grumbled as she tried to work her way to James's side.

"They're Houston's soldiers, James," Hannah said.

"You two stay put," James insisted. "I ain't seen 'em before."

Standing eye to eye with James, Miss Barrington whispered, "They've asked our permission to camp here for the night, and I've invited them to supper."

"Supper!" James wrinkled his brows together in a scowl and spat.

Miss Barrington shuddered. "I don't mean to be rude, James, but spitting is a horrible habit."

"Supper doesn't sound too dangerous." Hannah giggled. The girls inched their way around James to get a better view of the Tejanos.

Still unconvinced, James gripped his rifle tightly and clenched his jaw. He glowered at the intruders.

The man on the lead horse dismounted and slid his rifle into a scabbard on the side of the horse's saddle. His spurs jingled against the ground as he walked toward James. *"Señor, yo soy Capitán Juan Seguín."* He held out his hand.

"Juan Seguín," Hannah mumbled. "He's in our history book."

Jackie tugged excitedly at Hannah's sleeve. "He's famous, Hannah! Can we get his autograph?"

Both girls giggled until James glared at them. "Hush now. They may be with . . . ah . . . you-know-who's army." His voice lowered with the last few words.

"The captain doesn't speak English, James," Miss Barrington said in the same soft tone, "but he says he's been around the Texians long enough to understand quite a bit of it."

Red-faced, James coughed and muttered under his breath. "Why in tarnation didn't ya tell me that?"

Captain Seguín nodded and held his hand toward James again.

"James, he's on your side," Hannah said.

"Come on," Jackie encouraged. "We want to meet Juan Seguín."

Attempting to straighten out her windswept hair, Miss Barrington smiled brightly. "James, they're waiting for your answer."

James frowned at Miss Barrington as he lowered his rifle. "All right, all right, missy. Don't git yer feathers ruffled." James reached out and shook hands with Captain Seguín. "Pleased to meet ya, I reckon."

"Mucho gusto, señor." Although Captain Seguín smiled, his eyes were still on James's rifle.

"Maybe one of them fellers can help me with the butcherin'," James mumbled. Miss Barrington took James's arm and led him over to the other men, who were still on horseback. "These are three privates from Seguín's company: Antonio Cruz, Pedro Herrera, and Manuel Tarín." Each man nodded as his name was mentioned.

"Howdy, I'm James Wells," he said in a grumpy voice. "Can one of you fellers give me a hand with my hog?" Miss Barrington quickly translated his question.

The men spoke to one another and dismounted. Private Herrera walked toward the hog suspended beneath the tree.

James's mouth dropped open as Herrera pulled a knife from his boot. "Well, I'll be derned," James said. "He's fixin' to start without me! Miss Barrington, would ya mind fetchin' my cookin' gear from the wagon?" Not waiting for an answer, he hurried off after Herrera. The other men, except for Captain Seguín, led the horses to a grassy area.

Jackie tapped Miss Barrington's shoulder. "Have you forgotten we're here?" Jackie asked.

"Of course not," Miss Barrington said. "Captain Seguín, this is Jackie and Hannah."

"Mucho gusto." The captain smiled as he shook hands with the girls. His brown eyes were warm.

"Mucho gusto, Señor Seguín," Jackie murmured.

"Mucho gusto," Hannah repeated. The words felt strange on her tongue.

"Miss Barrington!" James hollered. "Y'all can lollygag later. I need my things."

Miss Barrington blushed. "I'll be right there, James." She grabbed a handful of her skirt to keep from tripping and hurried off to the wagon.

Seguín nodded to Hannah and Jackie. *"Con permiso, señoritas."* He turned and headed toward the horses.

"Hey, what's this?" Jackie bent down and turned up

Journey to San Jacinto

the bottom of her dress just enough to reveal several clusters of prickly stickers and burrs along the hemline. Frowning, she pulled a burr loose with her fingers. "Ouch! I'm not touching those spiky things again."

Hannah held her dress out to the side. "We must've picked them up while we were walking through all that grass."

"How do we get them off?" Jackie grabbed a handful of her skirt and shook it hard. Only one burr fell to the ground.

"Girls," Miss Barrington called out from inside the wagon, "that will have to wait. I need your help."

Hannah and Jackie hurried over to the wagon. Miss Barrington hoisted up a black cauldron from the wagon bed. "James will need this." She gave it to Hannah.

"It's heavy," Hannah said as she set it on the ground.

Miss Barrington handed Jackie a bucket. "Captain Seguín said there's a creek just through those trees on the left. Why don't you get some fresh water for our meal?"

"What's that big wooden barrel on the side of the wagon for?" Jackie asked.

"James mentioned it was almost empty," Miss Barrington said. "We'll have to refill it before we get started tomorrow."

Hannah dragged the heavy cauldron over to James, and then the girls headed for the creek. "I think Miss B has a little crush on Captain Seguín," Jackie giggled. "Did you see the way she looked at him?"

Hannah laughed. "That's probably why she sent us for water. She wants to keep us busy."

They continued to snicker and gossip about Miss Barrington until they finally found the creek. It had swollen to the size of a river. Tall cypress trees and bushes lined the banks. Some of the trees sprang up from the depths of the water.

Humming "Oh Susanna," Hannah strolled along the river, admiring the beauty of the land. Tiny white flowers flourished in the patches of grass graced by sunlight. Gray squirrels scrambled through the trees, flicking their tails as they chased each other.

With the bucket in one hand, Jackie balanced herself on the roots of a large tree on the river's edge. She tiptoed delicately over the top of the longest root like a circus performer on a tightrope. Once she was out from the shoreline, Jackie crouched down and gathered her dress around her legs. She dipped the bucket in the water and set it next to her. Suddenly, her face lit up as she pointed at the bushes on the shoreline. "Look Hannah, kitties! Aren't they adorable?"

"Don't move, Jackie!" Hannah yelled. "There's something with a long tail in that tree."

Jackie glanced up at the leafy branch in the tree next to her. The furry tail twitched. A sleek, dusty-colored ani-

Journey to San Jacinto

mal crept gracefully out on the limb. It hissed and growled at Jackie.

"It's a big cat . . . with really pointy teeth!" Jackie shrieked. The cougar adjusted its hind legs on the branch and lowered its head.

"Be brave, Jackie! She's only protecting her kittens!"

"HELP!" Jackie's terrified scream echoed through the countryside.

Unexpectedly, the cougar leaped toward Jackie. She fell backward into the deep river. The cougar landed with deadly accuracy on the exact spot where Jackie had been perched, knocking the bucket into the river. Ears pinned back, the cougar snarled as it raised a front paw and batted at Jackie. Jackie's arms and legs splashed wildly, and then everything became still. Jackie was gone.

Horses' hooves pounded from behind Hannah as the crack of a rifle split the air. The cougar darted into the thick bushes.

Captain Seguín and Private Cruz, riding on horseback, neared the edge of the rushing water. Seguín aimed a pistol toward the bushes. Cruz searched for signs of the camouflaged predator slinking along in the tangled undergrowth.

"There was a cougar and Jackie fell in the river!" Hannah stammered. "She's gone!"

"Nosotros la encontraremos," Captain Seguín assured her.

"I don't understand you," Hannah said nervously.

Private Cruz pointed downstream, guiding his horse into the water. The two men rode on ahead.

"Tarnation, what's all the ruckus 'bout?" James barked as he hiked into the clearing. "Y'all are gonna bring Santa Anna's army down on all of us if yer not careful! Where's yer friend, and who shot the rifle?"

Hannah's heart pounded. "Jackie fell in the river when a cougar attacked. Captain Seguín and the other guy, Private Cruz, rode after her."

"Don't give up on yer friend," James said soothingly. "She's a spunky little gal."

Hannah called out Jackie's name as she and James followed the meandering river. The farther downstream they went, the faster the current moved. And there was no telling how deep it became as it grew wider.

"What if the cougar finds her first?" Hannah's voice trembled.

"Don't borrow trouble, missy. We ain't seen no bad signs yet." James pointed to a thick growth of trees. "Here comes someone now!"

Two horses emerged, bearing three riders. Captain Seguín held Jackie in front of him on the saddle. Private Cruz was carrying the bucket.

Hannah and James followed the horses and riders back to camp. Private Cruz gently eased Jackie down from Captain Seguín's horse. Jackie wrapped her arms around herself and shivered. Grime clung to her skin and wet clothing, and water dripped from her dress.

"I'll get her a blanket," Miss Barrington said. She hurried off to the wagon.

Jackie's face had turned the color of a pale moon, contrasting vividly with her tangled black hair. She touched a large bruise on her forehead and groaned, "I feel kinda dizzy." A sticky red substance was seeping through the yellow fabric of her sleeve.

"What happened to your arm?" Hannah gasped.

Jackie gazed at the blood in disbelief and collapsed to the ground.

CHAPTER SEVEN

❧❧

Nick and the Mexican Army

The sky darkened, and so did Nick's thoughts. He fidgeted from side to side on the saddle. They had been on the road for more than an hour, and the slow rocking gait of the horse was becoming uncomfortable. "General Castrillón, how much farther are we going?" Nick asked. "I think your horse is hungry."

"My horse, you say?" The general chuckled. "It seems you have finally found your tongue."

"It's the only part of me that's not numb. Seriously, General, you should put some padding on this saddle."

General Castrillón observed the men marching beside him. Their heads hung down, and their shoulders sagged. "Would you prefer to walk and carry a heavy pack?"

"Come to think of it, the view is much better up here."

The general chuckled again. "Very well, Nicholas. You are not afraid to speak your mind. I like that."

Nick stretched his arms, trying to work the kinks out of his back. "I have a sister who doesn't."

"Where is your sister?"

"I was looking for Hannah and her friend when you found me."

"Your countrymen have scattered all over *Tejas,* running from us like frightened rabbits. Your sister could be anywhere."

"I know," Nick sighed. "She's a real pain."

A dark cloud spilled over the edge of the horizon. Nick recalled the cloud of dust the Mexican soldiers had stirred up earlier. "General Castrillón, is part of your army up ahead?"

"No, my young friend. We are about to find ourselves in a tempest."

"A tempest?"

"A storm as strong as His Excellency's army. We will stop soon. Did you think I had not noticed the haggard look of my men?"

"Nothing gets past you," Nick said solemnly.

"Listen carefully, Nicholas," General Castrillón warned. "By morning, we will join another unit. I suggest you keep that hat down tightly on your head, especially if other officers are present. I would not want them to get a glimpse of those blue eyes of yours."

"I'm kinda young to be a threat."

"I see you as a boy in an extremely precarious position. His Excellency will view you as the enemy."

Nick felt his throat tighten. The general was right. He would have to take precautions if he wanted to stay alive. "What about your men?" Nick asked.

"They are merely curious. The gossip of their general picking up a young *norteamericano* has spread throughout the ranks as fast as fire through a dry field."

Thunder crackled and exploded above their heads, sounding like a dozen cannons firing at some unseen enemy. The sky changed from a deep blue to an ominous black, and cold wind filled with drizzle splattered across Nick's face. The soldiers picked up their pace.

Cesar whinnied nervously, rearing up as General Castrillón pulled back on the reins. The general spoke gently to his horse to calm him.

Drizzle became rain, falling in gray sheets. Water washed across the land in rippling streams, and rain poured off Nick's hat as if a spout had opened over his head.

In the distance, silhouettes of buildings appeared out of the gloom. The general urged his horse closer as Nick followed. The buildings were mere skeletons, rickety frameworks rising up from ashes. A streak of lightning presented a clearer picture—most of the buildings had been burned to the ground.

"Were they struck by lightning?" Nick asked.

"I suspect it was your countrymen who set fire to those buildings," General Castrillón replied. "We have been through several settlements, and I have seen total devastation of Texian property. It is such a waste."

"No way."

"Yes, Nicholas. They know the Mexican army is coming, and in their haste, they have left homes and fields abandoned. Some go so far as to destroy everything in sight before they flee. Their desire is to leave nothing behind that could be of any use to our army. Ahh . . . look up ahead."

The general guided his horse toward a farmhouse. The home was two stories tall with an immense barn behind it. A flowerbed surrounded the home, creating a path to the front, and a line of shade trees bordered the yard.

As the rain slowed to a sprinkle, the general and Nick dismounted in the front yard. An open door banged in the wind. General Castrillón handed the reins of his horse to a soldier, and they stepped over the threshold into the abandoned house. As Nick followed the general into a dark room, something crunched beneath his soggy boots.

Lightning flashed, revealing a fireplace. A soldier quickly passed by Nick and lit a fire. Light danced on the wallpaper, which had a pattern of soft pink flowers. The fire crackled and popped while it devoured the kindling.

Awed by the destruction around him, Nick stood motionless. Broken furniture and dishes littered the floors. Torn rose-colored drapes swirled in velvety heaps beneath the windows. A once-magnificent home was now in shambles.

Nick bent down to pick up a painting from the floor. He held it toward the light. Two small children and their mother were dressed in their Sunday best. They smiled, but the woman's eyes haunted him. Feeling like a trespasser, he turned the painting over and leaned it against the wall.

Despite the warm drafts of air circulating through the room, Nick still felt cold. He cupped his hands together and blew into them. His wet clothing clung to him as drops of water pooled beneath his feet.

General Castrillón removed his hat and relaxed on the only chair in the room left intact. It was a beautifully carved rocker made from golden oak. "Do not look so dismal, Nicholas," the general said. "We should be grateful the owners could not bear to burn this house down."

A younger soldier approached General Castrillón. He had a clean-shaven appearance with straight dark hair and light brown eyes. His uniform matched those worn by the marching soldiers.

General Castrillón rocked back in the chair and spoke to the young soldier in Spanish. Then the general turned to Nick and said, "This man is Miguel. He will show you the proper way to groom my horse. When you are finished, report back to me. Do you understand?"

"Yes, sir," Nick responded glumly. He followed Miguel outside. The rain had finally stopped. The storm was moving away. Soldiers were beginning to pitch their tents on the highest ground they could find.

Several horses were sheltered beneath the green canopy of an old oak. Miguel pointed to Cesar, and they approached the stallion. The horse was munching contentedly from a feedbag. Nick patted Cesar while Miguel removed a brush from a bag he carried and started to groom the horse. After a few minutes, he spoke softly to Cesar and handed Nick the brush.

Nick brushed down the horse's flanks in long smooth strokes. He couldn't help remembering the other times he had worked with horses. His family liked to vacation at dude ranches in the hill country north of San Antonio, and Nick hung around the wranglers until they finally put him to work. Handling horses came easily to him.

As he groomed Cesar, Nick noticed a group of spectators forming nearby. They were the same soldiers who had found him in the tree and pointed their bayonets at him.

A short, stout man with a bushy black mustache strutted over to Nick. He spoke Spanish in a high-pitched raspy voice. *"¡No lo estás haciendo bien!"*

"Huh?" Nick muttered.

The man's eyes twinkled as he smiled broadly, revealing the gap between his two front teeth. He shook his head as if something was very wrong. Using excessive hand motions, he pointed this way and that as he rambled on. When he finished, he let out an exasperated sigh, rolled his eyes, and paraded before Nick with his hands on his hips. The other soldiers chuckled at the man.

Nick continued to brush Cesar's neck. He tried his best to ignore the man, but the short soldier stopped beside him. *"Deja enseñarte."* He jerked the brush from Nick's hand and began to groom the horse.

Nick smirked as he stepped back. "Yo dude, don't get too close to that horse."

The soldier glanced curiously at Nick, shrugged, and patted the horse on the side. Suddenly Cesar's head swung around. Snorting angrily, the horse reared up. Prancing sideways, Cesar quickly knocked the short man down. He landed with a thud on his back, his feet pointed skyward.

"¡Oye, Montaño! ¿Qué pasó?" a soldier called out, laughing

at the man on the ground. The other men chuckled even harder at the horse's actions.

Montaño tried desperately to roll away from the horse, but Cesar wasn't finished. The stallion moved forward and pawed at the frightened man.

Quickly Nick rushed forward, grabbed Cesar's reins, and led him away. "There, boy, it's all right," he said soothingly.

Montaño jumped to his feet. His chest heaved as he struggled to catch his breath. With a sheepish expression, he approached Nick and held out his hand. Nick understood this language; Montaño was offering a gesture of peace. Nick gave a sideways smile and shook his hand.

"*Gracias,*" Montaño said.

"No problem, dude," Nick responded.

The show was over. Montaño followed his comrades back to their camp. Miguel finished picking up the horse's gear and motioned for Nick to follow him back to the house. Nick gave Cesar one last scratch between his ears. "See ya tomorrow, boy."

Inside the house, Nick remained in the shadows by the door. The clutter had been cleaned up and tall white candles illuminated the room. A long table stood near the fireplace. Several officers conversed while they studied maps strewn about the table.

General Castrillón had already changed into dry

clothes. As he rocked back in the chair, he spoke to Miguel before gesturing for Nick to draw nearer. "It seems you have done an excellent job with my Cesar. This will be one of many duties assigned to you."

Nick grimaced at the thought of doing chores for the Mexican army. "Did Miguel tell you about the guy and your horse?"

"Of course, Nicholas. He told me all about the buffoon who tried to get too close to my horse." General Castrillón smiled. "Cesar taught him a lesson he will never forget. As for my men, you will soon be considered one of them."

What does that mean? Nick thought.

The general picked up a bundle of clothes from the floor beside him. "Put these on until yours are dry. Miguel will find you something to eat and a place to sleep. Tomorrow will be another long day."

Nick was too exhausted and hungry to worry about the next day. He stuffed the clothes under his arm and followed Miguel through the house, exactly as the general had ordered.

CHAPTER EIGHT

⊰ː ⊱

The Camp

When Jackie woke up, she found Hannah, Miss Barrington, and James buzzing around her. Hannah wiped the dirt from Jackie's face, Miss Barrington finished tying a bandage around her arm, and James added plenty of kindling to the fire. The flames flickered and popped, sending warm light into the shadowy darkness. Night had fallen. The air smelled of an approaching storm.

"What happened?" Jackie asked weakly.

Hannah helped Jackie sit up. "You fainted—twice."

Jackie shivered. "The sight of blood really creeps me out—especially my own blood. Do you have any lip gloss, Hannah? My lips are really dry."

"Sorry, wrong century," Hannah said. "How are you?"

Jackie tried to comb her tangled hair with her fingers. "My arm stings a little."

Miss Barrington lifted up Jackie's arm to examine her handiwork. Strips of white cloth formed crude bandages, covering the deep scratch marks left by the cougar. "Captain Seguín gave me an herbal remedy to keep the cuts from getting infected," Miss Barrington explained.

"Cuts, as in more than one?" Jackie's eyelids fluttered as she swayed back.

"Gotcha," James said. He caught Jackie just before she tumbled over and eased her back up. "That cougar left its mark on ya, but you'll be righter than rain soon 'nough. Seems it grabbed yer arm with its razor-sharp claws and—"

"That's enough," Miss Barrington interrupted.

James prodded the fire with a long stick. "I know'd a feller who tangled with a wildcat. He got all cut up and come down with the fever. Doctor in town had to bleed 'im."

"What?" Hannah asked.

"The doc opened up a vein in his arm to let the bad blood out." James tossed another piece of wood into the fire.

"Gross," Jackie mumbled. She pulled her injured arm close to her body.

"James," Miss Barrington scolded, "you may discuss all those gory details later."

James grunted as he rose to his feet. "Tarnation, jest wanted to make sure the little gal was better. Best tend to my vittles if I ain't needed here no longer." He stomped over to the wagon, removed three wooden boxes, and set them beside the fire. "Y'all can sit on these." He mumbled a few more words about being unappreciated and skulked back toward a second fire he used for cooking food.

Sighing, Miss Barrington handed some clothes to Jackie. "I scrounged up an old pair of pants and shirt you can wear until your dress dries. Here's a rope to hold those pants up. Better hurry, that lightning keeps getting closer."

Hannah helped Jackie to her feet, and they climbed up into James's wagon. Stacks of wooden crates, wooden kegs, and stuffed cloth bags almost filled the wagon bed. Jackie pushed a few boxes aside as she walked to the back to change her clothes.

Hannah gazed out at the stars. "Sorry I dragged you into this time-travel thingy again," she said, twisting a strand of hair around her finger.

"That's okay," Jackie said quietly. "Friends are supposed to be there for each other."

Still feeling guilty, Hannah searched the sky. Through

an open patch in the clouds, she spotted the Big Dipper. "When we were back in the classroom, I saw two words appear in the dust on the trunk. One was *HANNAH,* and the other was *HELP.*"

"I knew you were way too eager to open that trunk."

Hannah looked at her ring. She turned it around and around on her finger. "I think it's Mr. Barrington who needs our help."

"Hannah."

"What?"

"Forget about Mr. B. This outfit is a total disaster!" Jackie exclaimed as she marched to the front of the wagon.

Hannah covered her mouth to stifle a giggle. "It's not that bad."

Jackie's pants, rolled up from the bottom, were at least four sizes too big. Her shirt hung down almost to her knees. "I look like a hillbilly! Don't you ever, ever, ever let Miss B choose clothes for me again."

"I promise," Hannah laughed.

As the girls climbed out of the wagon, Miss Barrington took Jackie's dress and hung it from a tree branch near the fire so it could dry. James hurried toward them, balancing two tin plates in one hand and a third in the other. He was grinning from ear to ear. "Them Tejanos have finished seconds and are already askin' fer more!" He glanced at Miss Barrington with his shoulders back, his nose a little higher than usual. "They appreciate my cookin', missy."

Miss Barrington smiled brightly. "It smells simply delicious, James. We're extremely lucky to be traveling with such a talented chef."

James blushed as he handed Jackie and Hannah their plates. Steam rose off the chunks of meat covered in gravy. At the edge of each plate was a huge, mouthwatering biscuit.

"Thanks, James," Hannah said. She immediately took a bite of the warm biscuit. The girls giggled as James gave the last dish to Miss Barrington and scurried off. All three sat down beside the fire.

"This is as good as my nana's *guisado,*" Jackie admitted. "And she's a terrific cook."

Gazing over at the other campfire, Hannah watched the Tejanos. Captain Seguín sat near the fire, reading a letter. Private Tarín pulled out a guitar from a pack and began strumming a Spanish ballad. His voice lifted through the camp with an aching sadness. As he sang, Hannah relaxed. She wished she could understand the words. Private Herrera had already finished assembling one tent and was shaking out a large canvas for another.

Private Cruz approached Miss Barrington and hunched down beside her. He looked younger than Hannah's father. The edges of his pant legs were frayed and uneven, and his jacket had patches sewn on the arms. A blue beaded rosary adorned his hatband, the cross swinging loosely to the side. The man spoke softly in Spanish to

Miss Barrington while Jackie and Hannah devoured their meal.

"He's one of your rescuers," Hannah whispered excitedly to Jackie. "He and Captain Seguín came galloping up on horseback and shot at the cougar. They're like knights without the shining armor."

Jackie's eyes shone with admiration. "I thought that only happened in movies."

"It was so cool," Hannah sighed.

"I remember someone pulling me out of the river and . . . there were horses. It's all a little fuzzy."

Hannah dipped her biscuit in the gravy. "He's your hero, Jackie."

Jackie leaned forward. "Private Cruz, *gracias*—ah, I can't think of the right words in Spanish. Thanks for rescuing me."

The man stood up. He walked around Miss Barrington and gently grasped Jackie's hand as he smiled at her. *"Me da mucho gusto que te sientas mejor."*

Hannah watched Private Cruz walk away, and then she nudged Jackie. "What did he say?"

Jackie wrinkled her brows as she thought. "Something like he's happy I'm better."

Miss Barrington moved her box closer to the girls. "He's been checking on you since they brought you back to camp. He has a wife and two children he misses dearly.

These Tejano soldiers wear their courage like a badge of honor. I don't think I've met anyone quite like them." Miss Barrington looked off into the distance. "They're extremely gallant."

Hannah scraped up the last of her meal. "I feel safer with them around."

Miss Barrington delicately separated a chunk of meat into bite-sized pieces. "They'll fight for what they believe in. Most of these men were born here, in Texas. This is their land. Seguín's family has lived here for generations. Think about it, girls. Their spirit . . . their tenacity and determination have helped make Texas what it is in our own time."

Hannah set her plate down and held her hands toward the fire to warm them. "I wonder what happened to Nick?"

"Who knows?" Jackie said. "If Nick's here, he's all by himself."

"Girls, let's keep our thoughts positive," Miss Barrington encouraged. "We don't know if Nick is even in this century."

"I guess so," Hannah said trying to sound convincing. But she couldn't shake off the feeling that something had gone dreadfully wrong, and Nick was in serious trouble.

CHAPTER NINE

The Drummer Boy

As a yellow sun peeped lazily over the horizon, the camp awakened full of sound. The hum of voices mingled with mockingbird songs. A loud bugle call boldly announced morning duties. The Mexican army stirred and grumbled as they stretched their stiff, sore muscles.

The smell of steaming coffee drifted upstairs. Nick had spent the night on the floor at the end of the hallway. He wished that he was in his own bed, and that the familiar aroma was his mother's cooking.

"Nicholas."

Nick rolled over and cracked an eye open. It was Miguel. "I hate mornings," Nick said quietly. He reluctantly put his hat on and trailed Miguel down the stairs and out the front door.

Deep, muddy puddles had formed across the lawn. A large brass cannon stood at the edge of the yard. Everything seemed strangely in place, including the soldiers.

Nick and Miguel rounded the corner of the house and continued until they reached a corral beside the barn. A saddle and bridle hung over the top rail of the fence. The tools for grooming Cesar were on a dry patch of ground beneath the saddle. Miguel pointed toward the horses, mumbled something in Spanish, and walked away.

Yawning, Nick bent over to pick up the brush—and caught sight of his clothes. He wore an old uniform, a Mexican soldier's uniform! His faded blue jacket was trimmed with a red collar and cuffs. The stained trousers were loose, but the fit was similar to his jeans. Last night, he had been too exhausted to care what he had changed into as long as it was dry. Now in the morning light, there was no mistaking how he was dressed. "This is wrong on so many different levels," Nick muttered.

Nick spotted Cesar among the horses belonging to the general's staff. He was a magnificent animal, towering over the other horses by several inches. As if sensing his importance, Cesar kept his distance from the other horses. When one of them drew near, he snorted and pawed the ground arrogantly as if to say, "I am the general's horse. I will soon carry an important man into battle."

Ignoring the glances of the soldiers, Nick whistled

loudly. Cesar pricked up his ears as Nick dropped the saddle on the other side of the fence. He grabbed a rail and climbed up, sitting on the top rung. Cesar pranced over, expecting attention. "Okay, boy," Nick said. "I'll take good care of you."

Nick placed the bridle over Cesar's head and scratched him between his ears. Then he jumped to the ground and picked up the wire brush. He groomed the animal and centered the saddle on his back, cinching it tightly beneath the horse's belly.

A man waved to Nick from behind the fence. It was Montaño. Nick wound Cesar's reins around the saddle horn. The horse snorted arrogantly at Montaño and reared up on his hind legs in a threatening pose. Nick chuckled as Montaño backed away from the corral. Cesar shook his head and trotted into the center of the horses, scattering them like marbles across a slick floor.

Montaño waved again. Nick was cautious but curious. He climbed over the fence, and together they headed toward the campsites.

The white canvas tents looked like ships' sails in a sea of green grass. Smoke from the campfires wafted up, carrying a spicy scent of sizzling food. There were women in long skirts cooking at some of the campfires. Nick hadn't noticed them before. What were women doing in the Mexican army?

When Nick and Montaño reached the middle of the encampment, Nick recognized the other soldiers. They were the same ones who had laughed at Montaño the night before. Several nodded in approval as Nick approached them. Montaño attempted to straighten out any wrinkles in Nick's jacket, dusting off the shoulders while he spoke Spanish in short crisp syllables. Another man handed Nick a tin cup of coffee and gestured for him to sit by the fire.

Everything smelled so mouthwateringly good that Nick felt his stomach rumble. He hoped a meal would follow the coffee. Soon a plate containing a meager amount of shredded meat and beans was set in Nick's hands.

The men served themselves and talked as they ate, enjoying the company of friends. Nick had been silently accepted into the fellowship by the time he had gobbled up his food. Thoughts of warfare became momentarily forgotten while they savored the last of the coffee.

A boy about Nick's age joined the group. The boy was shorter than Nick, and he carried a snare drum at his side. *"Buenos dias,"* the boy said, glancing curiously at Nick. His face looked strangely familiar. In fact, he looked like Montaño.

The men greeted the boy as he carefully set his drum and drumsticks on the ground. Montaño filled a plate with what was left of the food and handed it to the boy.

It reminded Nick of the time he had gone on a fishing trip with his father, uncle, and cousins. The similarities and differences started to twist together like the fibers in a rope. But this wasn't a fishing trip; it was war.

When the men finished eating, they began to check their weapons. Montaño swabbed out the barrel of his musket. Another man honed a knife to a sharp edge.

The boy tapped Nick's arm and motioned for him to follow. They jogged away from the tents to an open area. The boy pointed to himself. *"Soy Diego."*

Nick smiled broadly. "I'm Nick."

Diego pulled from his pocket a medium-sized ball fashioned from rags and scraps of leather sewn together. He eagerly showed it to Nick. Nick raced ahead several yards and held out his hands as Diego tossed the ball to him. After catching it, Nick spotted a slight rise to the land, similar to a pitcher's mound. He hustled over and stood atop it like his favorite Houston Astros player, Roy Oswalt. He wound up and threw the ball to Diego.

Diego laughed so hard at Nick's stance and technique that he bobbled the ball, dropping it to the ground. The boy from the past had never seen anything like it before. Now it was his turn. Concentrating on his target, Diego picked up the ball and imitated Nick's moves.

The ball soared through the air and snapped into Nick's hands. His eyes widened in amazement. "Yo dude, you're a natural," he called out.

With a devious smirk, Nick motioned for Diego to move back, and he hurled a spinning fastball. He could hear it pop into Diego's hands.

"*¡Ay! ¿Qué fue eso?*" Diego exclaimed as he gaped at his reddening hands.

Nick snickered. "Bring on the heat, Diego!"

"*¡Aquí te va!*" Diego wound up and lobbed the ball through the air. But his enthusiasm suddenly turned to alarm as General Castrillón rode up on Cesar. He scowled at the boys as they approached him.

"It's my fault," Nick admitted as he hid the ball behind his back. "I should've gone back to the house after I ate breakfast."

General Castrillón's face was somber. "You cannot continue in this manner, Nicholas. The next time you will both be punished."

"Yes, sir," Nick gulped. Diego stood at attention, unflinching.

"Later today, we will be joining General Santa Anna, and you are expected to abide by my wishes. A soldier must learn to obey orders."

But I'm not a soldier, Nick thought.

"Now, explain to me, Nicholas, how do you acquaint yourself with my men so easily?" The corners of General Castrillón's mouth turned up in a slight smile. "Only yesterday, I allowed you to join us, and already my men have fed you. And now I find you with one of their sons."

The Drummer Boy

Nick shrugged. "I usually get along with just about anyone."

General Castrillón's smile faded. "Nicholas, I think it best to leave you under the care of my soldiers. You will march alongside your new friend. I cannot take the chance of Santa Anna questioning your background. Not long ago, I tried to intercede on the part of your countrymen, even if they were not as innocent as you."

"What happened?" Nick asked.

"I was there at the fall of the Alamo," the general said. "When the battle was over, there were several survivors, *norteamericanos.* I protected them and brought them before Santa Anna as captured prisoners. Alas, he had them executed. So you see, Nicholas, this is no time for disobedience."

"I guess I understand. General Castrillón, did you know there are ladies in the camp?"

"The army always has its camp followers," General Castrillón replied. "I have ordered them to remain behind, but some of the wives refused. They follow and look after their men. It is a difficult path they have chosen."

Montaño approached the boys and held his son's drum up. Trying to avoid his father's scalding stare, Diego took the drum and slipped the harness on. Montaño escorted Diego toward the hundreds of soldiers preparing to march.

"Go join them, Nicholas," the general commanded.

Nick nodded glumly. He knew that would mean marching all day instead of riding. He also realized this wouldn't be the right time to ask about his clothes. At least for now, it was best to dress like a Mexican soldier.

CHAPTER TEN

Heading East

"That blasted rain last night," James bellowed. Wedged in a deep, muddy hole, the rear wagon wheel refused to budge. James thrust his shovel into the sloppy dirt. He tossed the mud to the side and it plopped into a puddle. The dirty water splashed up on Hannah's dress.

"James!" Hannah stared at her dress. Splotches of mud were everywhere. She wiped the dirt off her face with her hand.

"Step away, Hannah," James ordered. The next shovelful of mud flew through the air. Hannah jumped back just in time.

"Here, let me help you." Miss Barrington tried to brush the mud off Hannah's dress.

"Our clothes are really gross," Jackie complained. "My dress smells like river water and campfire smoke." She marched up to James, waving her hands in the air. "Can you stop a minute?"

James glanced up from his work. "What ya need, missy?"

"Look at my dress. It's disgusting." Jackie held her arms out and spun around. There was dried blood on her sleeve and stains along one side of her dress. The hemline was wet and heavy with morning dew from the grass. "Can't we go to a nearby town and buy something new to wear? Please, James?"

Grunting, James picked up a shovelful of dirt. "You look jest fine. Y'all can wash yer clothes in the next river we come to."

"Ew." Jackie shuddered. "I can't believe I miss my mom's Maytag, and I hate laundry day!"

Hannah took Jackie's arm and guided her away from the cockeyed wagon. "James doesn't know what a Maytag is," Hannah whispered.

"What kind of world is this?" Jackie exclaimed.

James continued shoveling. Once the lower part of the wheel was almost visible, he nodded to Seguín. "I'm ready, Capt'n," James called out.

Captain Seguín took a firm grip on the harness of the lead horse. James, Private Cruz, and Private Herrera leaned their shoulders against the rear of the wagon and pushed. "Put yer backs into it, boys," James declared.

"*¡Ándale!*" Seguín shouted. The wagon lurched forward and then skidded back into the slippery hole. James stepped back and wiped his muddy hands on his pants. Private Tarín moved to the side of the wagon and gripped the edge tightly.

"*Otra vez,*" Private Cruz grunted.

James cleared his throat. "Push!" The men leaned against the wagon. Slowly, the wheels began to turn as the wagon wobbled and rolled up from the rut.

James stomped his feet, knocking off the caked-up mud from his boots. "I wanna thank you, boys." He shook hands with each of the men.

Hannah approached Miss Barrington. "We've been up for hours, and we've only made it a few feet away from camp," Hannah said softly.

"Getting stuck in the mud is worse than a flat tire," Jackie remarked. "How did people get anywhere in this century?"

Miss Barrington pushed her glasses higher on her nose and smiled. "It takes sheer determination."

James strutted over, grinning at his accomplishment. He brushed his dirty hands against his pants. "Houston's waitin' on us, ladies."

Seguín, Herrera, and Tarín mounted their horses and

James helped Jackie up behind Private Cruz. The Tejanos had a spare horse for Miss Barrington to ride, and Hannah climbed into the wagon next to James.

"What do you know about General Houston?" Hannah asked as the wagon bumped along. "My brother, Nick, might be with him."

"Houston's the commandin' officer over the entire Texas army."

Hannah brushed her hair behind her ears, trying to keep the wind from blowing it in her face. "Nick's only thirteen. He's not old enough to be in the army."

James spat a long stream of brown tobacco to the side of the wagon and wiped his mouth on his sleeve. "If yer brother's with Houston, he's in the army."

Hannah felt a chill run down her back. "Nick doesn't know anything about being a soldier."

"Don't worry, they'll train the boy fer somethin'. Houston's been backtrackin' eastward through Texas fer days, tryin' to rally the men, git 'em ready fer battle."

"I'm—I'm kind of scared for Nick—and all of you."

James's smile faded. "Santa Anna has one powerful army. Now, don't git me wrong. I ain't afraid of dyin' fer freedom, but I ain't gonna end up like my friends at the Alamo. Houston's bidin' his time, and that suits me fine so long as he don't go and stir up nothin' before I catch up to 'em."

"I admire you, James," Hannah said, surprising the rough frontiersman.

"What fer?"

"You stand up for what you believe in. You were left behind, and now you're trying your best to find the army. You could go another direction and leave Texas."

"I ain't a coward, missy. Besides, the men are dependin' on these supplies. If yer brother's with Houston, we'll find 'im soon enough."

Hannah pointed at some figures on horseback in the distance. "Who are they?" she asked.

"Looks to me like five riders movin' lickety-split this-a-way," James muttered, suddenly serious. "Git behind me and fetch that rifle from under the seat."

Hannah moved to the rear of the wagon. She shoved a crate behind James, sat down on it, and handed James his rifle.

As the riders came closer, James pulled back on the reins, slowing the horses. He kept a firm grip on his rifle as Captain Seguín and his men galloped ahead.

Shaggy beards covered the strangers' chins. Dark tangled hair reached their shoulders, making them look like a desperate group of outlaws in a western movie—only these men weren't actors.

Miss Barrington trotted up on her horse, slowing to the pace of the horses pulling the wagon. "Those men are part of Seguín's company. Three of them have been scouting the movements of the Mexican army. The other two were with Houston. The captain thinks they have important information."

James wrinkled his brow with a sour expression on his face. He spat toward the side of the wagon as he tightened his grip on the rifle. "Miss Barrington, you best have some palavers with them men and find out what they know. Look 'em deep in the eye. If they're fidgety, we may be in fer trouble."

Miss Barrington sighed. "There's no need to worry, James."

"I'll be the judge of that," James growled, pulling the hammer back on his rifle. "I'm totin' a load of gunpowder, and I'll be derned if I'll have it taken from me."

James reached over and swatted Miss Barrington's horse on the rump. The horse jumped sideways and jerked away from the wagon. Turning first to give him a frustrated look, Miss Barrington quickly overtook the horses pulling the wagon and galloped toward the men who had gathered in a group.

"Do you really think there'll be trouble, James?" Hannah asked. "Those guys seem to want the same thing you do."

"I don't feel right dependin' on folks I know nothin' about. It jest don't set right with me." James pulled up on the reins, bringing his team of horses to a stop.

Hannah climbed to the front of the wagon and sat next to James. "Someday everyone in Texas will be grateful for what you're doing. You'll all be heroes in our eyes."

James chuckled. His eyes crinkled at the corners when he smiled. "Right purty words, Hannah. Right purty words."

Miss Barrington galloped back to the wagon. "We have to get moving immediately. Houston is just outside of Harrisburg, and the army is about to finish crossing Buffalo Bayou. We're not too far behind."

As he eased the hammer on his rifle back down, James said, "Well, that's the first good news I've heard in a long time."

"There's more, James. After Santa Anna burned Harrisburg to the ground, he headed for New Washington," Miss Barrington explained. "So if we don't hurry, the Mexican army will catch up to Houston before we do."

James watched a hawk in the distance. It circled and dove. Its talons opened as it shadowed a fleeing ground squirrel. "The varmint's done made his move then," James mumbled. "I reckon Houston will try to hold the higher ground once he reaches the San Jah-sen-ta River. It's as good a place as any."

San Jacinto, Hannah thought. *That's where we'll find Nick and Mr. Barrington.*

Journey to San Jacinto

"Seguín did mention that Santa Anna had split his army," Miss Barrington explained. "They're not traveling as one large group."

"That settles it." James snapped the reins and the horses stirred. "No time fer dawdlin'. The battle's purty near on us!"

CHAPTER ELEVEN

The Snake

Burned to the ground—all of it! Nick couldn't believe what he had just witnessed as they marched away from the still-smoldering ashes. After covering countless miles in the morning, the Mexican army had finally stopped for a break and to Nick's dismay, burned the entire town of Harrisburg. There was not one thing he could do except stand back and watch the hungry fire consume building after building, home after home. The destruction of an entire community had been accomplished with the mere wave of a hand from the ruthless dictator Santa Anna.

The faces of the men Nick marched beside showed no remorse for what they had done at Harrisburg. The Mexican army wanted to keep the Texian rebels from coming back and to scare others away, but to watch the chaos was overwhelming. The army had taken anything of value that could be carried away. Whatever was left was crushed, broken, shattered, or burned.

The next afternoon they reached New Washington. Santa Anna paraded his horse along the lines of men, assessing the strength of his army. He was dressed in an immaculate uniform. There was a hard look on the powerful man's face.

After a short break, they marched out of town. Nick remembered General Castrillón's warning. If his identity were revealed, he'd be in serious trouble. He pulled his hat down tightly and tried to let the rhythm of Diego's drum keep his thoughts under control.

Nick's feet started to hurt as they crossed through the countryside. It felt like there were small pebbles in his boots. Some of the soldiers around him wore only sandals, and others had no shoes at all. At least he had boots.

Nick turned to Diego. "Dude, where are we going?" Diego only shrugged.

"Don't we ever take breaks?" Nick asked.

Diego shrugged again.

"I have this sister, Diego. And if I ever find her—well, she's gonna learn the meaning of the word *payback*."

Diego smiled.

A bugle played the signal to halt. Like dominos toppling down upon one another, the soldiers dropped to the damp ground from exhaustion.

"Santa Anna probably treats his horses better," Nick mumbled to himself as he removed his boots and socks. Painful blisters had formed on the soles of his feet from the ill-fitting boots he had once considered comfortable.

Diego nudged Nick and handed him a large gourd. *"¿Quieres agua?"* Diego asked.

"Thanks," Nick mumbled as he sat up. He grabbed the gourd and drank from it in large gulps. Diego laughed as water spilled down the front of Nick's uniform. It didn't matter that it tasted bitter. Nick had never been this thirsty, even after football practice.

Next, Diego broke off a dried section of something resembling a biscuit and handed it to Nick. *"Aquí está, dude."*

Nick's eyes popped open. "Dude, you're learning English! Excellent." Nick felt his stomach rumble as he took a bite of the mystery food. He made a face. It had absolutely no flavor. He held his breath, took another bite, and tried to swallow.

Diego finished his half and stood up, motioning for Nick to follow him. Nick stuffed his socks into his boots and rose to his feet, sliding the remaining food into his pocket. His whole body ached as he picked up his boots and ran barefoot after Diego. They headed toward the back of the line of men, away from the watchful eyes of Diego's father.

There was a swampy area off to one side of the army. Low bushes, cattails, and tall reedy plants bordered a large slough. A chorus of croaking frogs blended in with the drone of insects. Ducks bobbed their heads in the water, searching for food.

Nick and Diego darted into the heavy brush. The ground became wet and slimy, and the cool earth felt good on the soles of Nick's feet. Farther out, he sank until gooey mud almost reached his ankles.

The sound of men's loud voices stopped the boys. They peered through the reeds. A group of impatient soldiers were arguing near the rear of the army. Their plain white cotton uniforms stuck to their backs, and their faces were shiny with sweat. They were attempting to move the large brass cannon, which slanted to one side, its wheels bogged down in the soft ground. The oxen strained against the yoke, trying to pull the cannon loose, but it refused to budge.

Nick trudged through the mud toward drier land, Diego following closely behind him. He spotted a shallow pool and waded through it to rinse his feet. Groups of silvery minnows darted away from him with each step he took. Nick shook the water off his feet, and they stepped up onto a drier spot. Slick wet mud bordered the bottoms of their pants.

"Mira." Diego said. Crossing the water was a gray snake. It was small, less than a foot long. The snake held its head

above the surface as it propelled itself through the water by moving its body back and forth. Once it reached the water's edge, the snake slithered onto a broad rock. It curved around itself, threw its head back, and opened its mouth wide. The inside of its mouth was white as cotton. Like a gray streak, the snake suddenly thrust its head into the reeds. When it pulled back, a pair of tiny green legs squirmed in the snake's partially closed mouth.

"Whoa," Nick muttered. "Hey, Diego, that's a cotton-mouth. They're really poisonous."

Diego looked puzzled.

"Cot-ton-mouth," Nick repeated more slowly.

"Co-ti-moth?"

"Yeah, that's close enough."

"Cotimoth," Diego said with confidence. "*Es una* coti-moth, dude."

Nick chuckled. "You got it."

There was a rustling noise in the bushes behind them. Nick looked toward the ground, and the noise stopped. Pestering insects hummed around his head. He shrugged, swatted at a mosquito, and took a step closer to the snake.

Nick broke off a tall cattail shooting up from the water. He touched the snake with the brown fuzzy end. "It can't bite us as long as it's swallowing that frog." Agitated, the snake moved over the rock and slipped into the reeds.

As Diego reached for a cattail, the rustling noise began

again. Nick turned to look behind him. Both boys froze. Diego's eyes opened wide in terror. "Cotimoth!"

About five feet away, a dark gray snake, much larger than the first, slunk through the grass. A wiggling black tongue emerged from its mouth, testing the air. "That's the granddaddy of all cottonmouths," Nick whispered.

Diego backed up. He motioned for Nick to follow him. The poisonous snake eyed Nick, never wavering from its spot. Nick held the cattail toward the snake to keep it from getting closer.

"No, Nick," Diego warned.

"I've got everything under control." Nick took a deep breath. As he tossed the cattail aside, the snake lunged at him!

BANG! The sound of a gun exploded in their ears. The cottonmouth dropped to the ground. Nick's heart pounded as he stared at the dead snake.

"Nicholas," General Castrillón scoffed from atop his horse, "why is it every time I turn around I find you getting into mischief?"

Nick exhaled with relief. The general slid a pistol into his belt and Cesar nervously pawed the ground.

Diego rushed forward and picked up the snake. With a broad smile on his face, he held it high like a trophy. The snake was almost as long as he was tall! Diego glanced anxiously from the snake to General Castrillón.

The general nodded. *"La víbora es tuya."*

Diego rushed off, trailing the snake behind him like the tail of a kite. *"¡Mira lo que tengo!"* he called out enthusiastically to the soldiers as he ran passed them.

"Thanks, General," Nick said. "You have perfect timing."

"You are welcome, Nicholas. I keep forgetting that you are but a boy. A boy who apparently needs much looking after." General Castrillón's eyebrows drew together. A dark look clouded his face.

"Have I done something else wrong?" Nick asked.

"No. You have been trying to play the part of a soldier, but you are not a soldier. Nicholas, what will you do after the Mexican army has defeated the rebels? Your family may no longer be in *Tejas* . . . or alive."

Nick lowered his eyes. There was a growing possibility that he would never find Hannah or get home.

"I can see you are troubled by these thoughts," General Castrillón acknowledged. "I am going to make you an offer. The military is no place for a boy. When we return to Mexico City, you may stay with my sister's family. They live on a large ranch in the country. It is a good life."

Nick stared at his feet and mumbled, "I'll think about it."

CHAPTER TWELVE

The Skirmish

"It feels like this pile of Popsicle sticks we're floating on is about to fall apart," Jackie complained. "If it sinks, we're goners."

"It's a ferry," Miss Barrington corrected. "Houston's entire army crossed Buffalo Bayou by ferry. This is the type of transportation they used in 1836." The ferry suddenly pitched to the side, causing boxes to shift across the wagon bed.

Jackie rolled her eyes. "They have a rope tied around a tree on both sides of the bank, and we're in the middle. The soldiers are pulling us across by hand! What if the rope snaps?"

"Shhh, they'll hear you." Hannah grabbed hold of the crate she was sitting on as the ferry bobbed through the water. "James said for us to stay quiet and out of sight. The other soldiers might make him leave us behind."

They heard a grating noise as something large scraped along the bottom of the ferry. As the wagon jerked forward, Jackie tumbled to the floor. "Hey!" She held up an index finger. "Rule number one while traveling: never get on a boat without a motor."

Hannah walked gingerly to the front of the wagon, touching the tops of the crates for balance. She peeked out as the ferry drifted across the bayou. The still water was murky, and dragonflies buzzed across the surface. A snowy white egret waded on black stick-like legs between the lily pads near the shore. Private Cruz was already on the other side, watching over the horses and waiting for them.

A line of five men on the ferry, including James, tugged at the rope tied to a tree, drawing them through the water. The ferry lurched as it came to a stop on the muddy shoreline. "We're here," Hannah announced cheerfully.

James hitched the horses to the wagon, and they continued on their journey. As soon as they distanced themselves from the ferry, Hannah moved to the front of the wagon and sat beside James. They stopped while Miss Barrington mounted her horse and Private Cruz helped Jackie up on his horse behind him.

As they followed the bayou east, the distant sound of drumming echoed throughout the prairie. "What's that, James?" Hannah asked.

"Reckon it's Santa Anna's army approachin' from the west," James snarled. "From the trail we're followin', Houston's camped up ahead on the rise. Jest past that's the San Jah-sen-ta River." James stopped the wagon in an oak grove and Hannah climbed down. "You gals best wait here whilst me an' Cruz take this ammunition to Houston."

Private Cruz helped Jackie off the horse. She straightened out her dress. "I'm starting to hate the outdoors. Isn't there a cabin around here, James? I could use a bubble bath."

"A bath with bubbles? Yer one funny gal," James chuckled. "Now stay put 'till I bring the wagon back."

Private Cruz looked at Jackie with concern. *"Hay muchas víboras y animales cerca del pantano."*

"What'd he say?" Hannah asked.

Miss Barrington put one arm around each girl. "He pointed out that there are many snakes and other creatures near the bayou. We might even spot an alligator."

"Lucky us," Jackie grumbled. "Something else with sharp teeth." She scanned the ground as James and Private Cruz rode away.

"Girls, in case you're interested, the city of Houston

will be founded a few miles west of here someday," Miss Barrington said.

"Houston's the home of the Galleria Mall," Jackie sighed. She had a dreamy look in her eyes. "All those stores, *and* an ice-skating rink."

"Let's stay focused. Right now we need to find Nick," Hannah said. "And don't forget, Mr. Barrington needs our help."

Miss Barrington fastened her horse's reins to a low branch. She gave Hannah a questioning look. "What makes you think my uncle is in trouble?"

Hannah bit her lip. "The words *HANNAH* and *HELP* appeared in the dust on his trunk back in the classroom. I think the message was there for a reason."

"You should have told me," Miss Barrington said with concern.

Hannah looked down. "I didn't think you'd believe me."

"Mr. B is probably up to his ears in trouble by now," Jackie added. "I'm even a teensy-weensy bit worried about Nick."

"You are?" Hannah stared in disbelief.

Jackie's eyes grew wide. "I'm not worried for him, I'm worried for *you*, Hannah. How will you explain to your mom and dad that a trunk sent your brother away for good?"

A sharp bugle call rang out and drums began to pound loudly. Curious, Hannah and Jackie started hiking toward the sound. Spanish moss hung from the trees like long dangling fingers, catching and clinging to their hair. As they reached an open area, they could see men from both armies. Cannons were being loaded.

"Those two cannons on the Texian side are called the Twin Sisters," Miss Barrington explained. On the opposite side sat a larger brass cannon. A Mexican artilleryman rolled a cannonball down its barrel.

Jackie's mouth fell open. "Look at all the Texians. Their clothes are worse than what we saw at the Alamo. Their pants are all muddy, and their hair, ugh. They look like wild men!"

"They're really angry," Hannah added. "They keep yelling at the Mexican soldiers."

Jackie pointed at the Mexican side. "Those guys over there on horses have such pretty red uniforms. Yikes, they're holding spears."

"That's the Mexican cavalry, and those spears are called lances," Miss Barrington said.

BOOM! BOOM! A double explosion from the Twin Sisters shook the land. A thundering roar echoed back from a single cannon on the Mexican side. Black plumes of smoky clouds spouted out from the artillery weapons as whistling cannonballs soared through the air.

Silently, the girls watched the cannons shake, rumble, and blast away at each other. "We're about to witness the birth of a free, independent nation—Texas," Miss Barrington said. "Brace yourselves, though. It'll be a massacre, only this time the Mexican army will be decimated. If I remember correctly, the battle itself is relatively short, only about eighteen minutes."

"Is this the actual battle?" Jackie asked.

"No, they're just sizing each other up," Miss Barrington said. "This is the skirmish that occurs the day before the battle. The Battle of San Jacinto takes place on April twenty-first, when Houston's soldiers catch the Mexican army by surprise."

"Ladies, I fetched the empty wagon back for y'all!" James exclaimed as he rushed toward them. "What the heck are ya doin' out here? I thought I left y'all back thar behind those trees."

"We just wanted to see what's happening, James," Jackie huffed. "They're shooting the cannons!"

BOOM!

"You want to know what's happenin'?" James shouted. "Them Sisters are lettin' that Mexican army have it with both barrels. We ain't got no cannonballs to speak of so they're jammin' all sorts of things in 'em, like horseshoes, chains, scrap metal. . . . Works purty good, if I do say so myself."

Across the field, Mexican officers in fancy plumed hats gathered around the cannon. They talked with each other, occasionally looking back at the Texians.

Scowling at the enemy, James spat and crossed his arms. "I met up with Seguín's brother-in-law, Sergeant Flores. He said Seguín had a mighty big talk with Houston before they crossed the bayou. Seems Houston wanted the Tejanos to stay out of the fight. He's scared his men would mistake 'em fer Mexican soldiers and shoot the lot of 'em. Seguín wouldn't have none of it. Houston's a big, tall man, kinda intimidatin' if you know what I mean, but Seguín, he wouldn't back down." James chuckled. "That Tejano has plenty of grit."

Suddenly there was silence. The cannons from both sides had stopped firing. "Finish your story, James," Miss Barrington insisted.

James sighed. "All right, all right, missy. Seems that most of Seguín's troops are from the San Antonio de Béxar area. They can't return home until Santa Anna is defeated. It's their battle as much as Houston's, so they come to terms. Seguín and his men agreed to put pieces of cardboard in their hatbands sayin' what side they're on. It's the most confounded thing I've ever heard tell of, but I reckon it'll work."

"James, have you seen my brother? Or Mr. Barrington?" Hannah asked.

"I was gittin' to that," he answered impatiently. "I haven't seen hide or hair of neither of 'em. After the battle, me an' Seguín'll help you gals look fer them." James turned back to the battlefield. "What in tarnation . . . ?"

The Mexican soldiers were rolling the brass cannon in reverse toward their camp as the Texians cheered wildly. The Twin Sisters had proven to be too much power for a single cannon to defend. "By George, it looks like they're backin' off," James declared proudly.

From the sideline, a group of Texians on horseback rode out onto the field, followed by half as many on foot. Hannah started counting. There were more than fifty.

The Mexican cavalry blazed in from the other side with polished swords and six-foot-tall lances. "Look at how they ride in nice straight lines," Hannah said.

"Thar a dangerous lot," James growled.

Shots rang out from the Texians' pistols. They paused to reload again. One Mexican cavalryman rushed ahead and caught a Texian in the shoulder with his lance. The young man flew off his horse, landing several feet to the rear. He lay motionless on the ground.

"They got him!" Jackie cried. "Is he dead, James?"

"Can't tell from here," James replied solemnly. "Now skedaddle on back to the wagon. The battlefield ain't a fittin' place fer ladies like yerselves."

Hannah swallowed hard. "Let's go. I've seen too much already." She turned to walk away.

Grabbing Hannah's arm, Jackie pointed toward the field. "Wait, Hannah!" she screamed. "He's alive! He's alive! Look, he's getting up!"

The young man had risen. He staggered at first, but then headed back to the Texian line on wobbly legs. "Well, I'll be," James muttered.

"Someone help him," Miss Barrington gasped, holding her hand to her heart. Rapid hoofbeats pounded across the field. The Mexican cavalry had also seen the resurrection, and they were swooping after him.

"Hurry, hurry, hurry," Jackie pleaded. The cavalry narrowed the gap, preparing to finish what they had started.

Miss Barrington pointed to the Texian side of the field. "Who is that rider?"

James shaded his eyes to get a better view. "Private Lamar. Jest look at 'im go." Lamar galloped up at breakneck speed and stopped in front of the young Texian soldier, blocking the path of the Mexican cavalry. Fearlessly, he shot his pistol at them and then took aim with a rifle. In a cloud of dust and horses, the cavalry turned to pull back.

Following Lamar's daring efforts, a second Texian on horseback rode up. Reaching down without stopping, he pulled the young man up to the back of his horse and rode safely to the Texian side.

"Hooray!" Hannah and Jackie cheered.

The Skirmish

Unexpectedly, several soldiers from the Mexican cavalry applauded the successful rescue mission. Lamar heard the applause; he whirled his horse around and bowed gallantly to the enemy before he rode away. Both armies broke off from the skirmish and returned to their sides.

"Why did they clap for their enemy?" Hannah asked.

"They respect Lamar's courage," Miss Barrington said.

"Suppose so," James grunted. "Houston's gonna be spittin' mad."

"But the guy was saved," Jackie reasoned.

James shook his head. "We're here to win this war, not to show off to one another. One side's clappin', and Lamar's bowin' to an audience like he's on a stage. We can't lose sight of our reason fer bein' here. Thar's too much at stake."

"I get it," Hannah said. "You'll have a hard time fighting each other if you start getting too friendly."

"That's right, little lady," James stated. "Yer absolutely right."

CHAPTER THIRTEEN

꙳ ꙳

The Battle

Under General Castrillón's orders many of the men, including Nick and Diego, worked through the night, building makeshift breastworks. They piled up saddles, brush, branches, crates, bags of corn and flour so high that Nick could barely see over the top. This lengthy barrier would protect them from flying musket balls once the battle began.

Good news arrived with the morning light. General Cos marched in with over five hundred soldiers. The additional troops were a welcome sight. Hundreds of white peaks from their tents stood out in patterns across the prairie. Cos's men were resting from the long march.

Yawning, Nick looked up at the sky as he tended to Cesar. "I hope this is my last duty for the day," Nick mumbled to the horse. "It's already afternoon. You think they'd give me a break."

Between the tents, Montaño and his friends were playing a game of cards. The serious hum of their voices, followed by Montaño's boisterous laughter, made Nick smile. Diego's father must be winning. The tempting smells of food simmering over the campfire reached him, and he took a deep breath. Diego would be back from his errand soon, and then they would eat.

As Nick brushed Cesar, he watched General Castrillón pacing through the camp. The general scowled at anyone who tried to talk to him. Several staff officers, including Miguel, trailed silently behind him like children waiting for a nod of approval from their father. General Castrillón ignored those following at his heels.

The general paused to speak with several *soldados* beside their large cannon, before finally approaching Nick. "I have not decided exactly what to do with you during this battle," the general admitted in a tense voice. "You are obviously not trained as a soldier, and I am not sure who you would shoot at even if I gave you a weapon." General Castrillón folded his hands behind his back and shook his head.

Nick glanced around at all the soldiers. "Don't worry about me, General. I'll stay back here out of everyone's way."

Journey to San Jacinto

"It may not be that easy, Nicholas. Our men are sandwiched between a swampy lake and a rabble of untrained, unpredictable *norteamericanos* who no longer have anything to lose from this war, and everything to gain. The terrain here is very different from where we have engaged the enemy in the past." General Castrillón cleared his throat as he surveyed the grassy land at the rear of the camp. "Houston is very clever for leading us to this swampy despicable piece of *Tejas* that is unfit for anything but breeding mosquitoes!"

Nick tried to recall everything he had learned at school about the Battle of San Jacinto. He knew Houston would be the victor, but he had no idea what would happen to any of the people he had met. "General, would you be . . . more careful . . . if you could somehow know the outcome of this battle?"

"I have been a soldier for many years, my young friend. I am always vigilant of my surroundings, but there are dangers." The general paused, focusing on the cannon. "I have never backed down from a battle, Nicholas. I expect the same of my men."

BOOM! BOOM! Sudden blasts from unseen cannons rocked the ground and parts of the breastworks exploded. Kernels of corn and flour from the shredded sacks flew skyward and rained down on the army.

Somewhere in the distance, a small fife-and-drum

band was playing. The music grew louder. Far beyond the breastworks, men marched down from a ridge in two long lines through the knee-high grass. The sounds of muskets and rifles firing overpowered the music. The Texians were upon them!

Spooked by the noise, Cesar reared up and freed himself from Nick's grasp. The frightened horse trotted away from the din.

"¡Prepárense!" General Castrillón roared. He grabbed Nick's shoulder. "Fall back to the lake. Follow it west. Don't stop until you are well out of range. Now go!"

"What about Diego?" Nick yelled as he backed nervously away.

"He knows what to do. Hurry!" the general warned.

Nick stared at General Castrillón shouting orders to the army. Some men picked up their muskets and fired at the oncoming enemy. Others frantically tried to locate their weapons as a Mexican bugler sounded the alarm. The camp was in an uproar as the Texians made their way closer to the holes in the breastworks. Shots rang out from every direction. Gunsmoke spread like a fog over the field, and many unarmed *soldados* collapsed to the ground, never to rise again. Loose horses and Mexican and Texian soldiers crisscrossed one another's paths in a mad rush.

Nick sprinted back toward the water, pausing to take

one last look at the horrendous scene he hoped to escape. General Castrillón was standing on a wooden crate next to the cannon. *"¡Fuego!"* a voice shrieked.

BOOM!

"Why is General Castrillón up there?" Nick cried out. "He's gonna get—"

The general directed the men beside the cannon and they fired it a second time. Black smoke swirled out of the mouth of the cannon and fell around the men like a shroud.

As the smoke parted, Nick saw General Castrillón fall to the ground. "No!" Nick choked. He couldn't turn away from the chilling scene. Shots echoed through the prairie and men screamed as Nick waited for the general to rise.

Heart pounding, Nick summoned his courage. He ran back toward General Castrillón. Suddenly, a soldier blocked his way. It was Miguel. Sweat trickled down Miguel's forehead, and he was panting. He grabbed Nick by the uniform, shoving him backward. Nick stumbled and fell to the ground. "Why'd you do that?" Nick demanded. "General Castrillón—he needs our help!"

As Nick got to his feet, Miguel pointed to the lake and roughly pushed him in the same direction a second time. *"¡Correle, muchacho! ¡Hay vienen los norteamericanos!"* Overhead, a shower of musket balls whistled past them.

Miguel dropped his musket to the ground. He angrily

grabbed Nick by the back of his uniform, dragged him several feet, and forcefully heaved him under a wagon like a sack of potatoes. Then Miguel retrieved his musket and disappeared into the battle zone.

Hugging the ground, Nick hid in the grass behind a wagon wheel. He saw men and horses running helter-skelter—some trying to take lives, some trying to stay alive. The screech of musket balls and cannon blasts, and the shouts of the men, started to blend together in an uneasy melody of discord.

Men's voices cried out over the land: "Remember the Alamo" and "Remember Goliad," along with *"Me no Alamo"* and *"Me no Goliad."* A storm of ammunition flew from all directions. It sounded like thunder. Nick closed his eyes tightly. Everything had been so different just a few minutes ago.

As he opened his eyes and stared between the spokes of the wheel, a large fearless man on a magnificent white stallion rode through the haze of spent gunpowder. The man wore tall leather boots, a dark coat, and a low three-cornered hat. He barked out orders to the Texians, his sword held high. "Sam Houston," Nick whispered. "It has to be him."

There was a blast like a large firecracker exploding, followed by a thud. Houston jerked back on his horse, clenching the reins tightly. He winced, reaching toward the lower part of his leg. The horse toppled to the ground with Houston trapped beneath it.

Three Texians rushed to Houston's aid. They quickly eased him out from under the dying animal. Others appeared, standing guard to protect their general, their rifles ready. Houston grimaced as they lifted him to his feet. He tried to stand, but his ankle couldn't support his weight.

Another man led a horse over to Houston and helped him mount it. As Houston raised his sword above his head, he shouted, "Stay the course, men! Victory is at hand!" He galloped away into the smoky air.

Scrambling out from under the wagon, Nick made a run for it. He joined a wave of *soldados* running away from the Texians. As Nick approached the lake, his feet started to sink into the swampy land, slowing his pace. It was as if the earth itself had grabbed hold of the Mexicans with muddy hands until the Texians could overpower them.

Many *soldados* waded knee-deep through the mud to reach the lake and attempted to swim away. But Texians on horseback swooped in from the left side, attacking in full force. More shots exploded from the Texians' pistols. The water in the lake turned a sickening shade of red, and bodies were scattered everywhere. The Texians were unstoppable and showed no signs of mercy.

Nick backtracked and ran west, just as General Castrillón had ordered. All of his football drills were being put to good use—only this time, he was running for his life.

Looking to the side, Nick noticed two Texians on horseback in the distance. One pointed at him. "They think I'm the enemy," Nick muttered. He dropped to the muddy ground, moving on his belly, reaching out hand over hand and trying to keep the grass from swaying too much one way or the other. The blades of grass and sharp pebbles chafed his hands, not that it mattered. He would have crawled over broken glass to find his way across this field and away from the horrors he had just witnessed.

Nick lifted his head from the mud. The two Texians on horseback rode slowly his way. They searched through the prairie grass as they came nearer. On the opposite side of Nick, only fifteen yards away, was a group of loose horses. Cesar was one of them. Nick rose to his feet and dashed toward the horses.

"There he is!" a man yelled.

BANG! There was a whistling noise and Nick's hat flew off his head.

"I'll get 'im!" a deep voice boomed.

BANG! Nick dove back into the grass and remained still. He pictured Hannah and Jackie finding his bloody, lifeless body on the ground. *When they find me full of bullets and bayonet wounds, it'll probably ruin their lives,* Nick thought to him-

self. They'll be so upset knowing they caused my death—they'll never fin-ish school, never go to a movie, never play video games, never go to Disney World, never ever eat pizza again because it was my favorite food, never . . .

"Over here, Hendrick," the first voice called out.

The grass swished as two horses stopped beside Nick. He slowly turned over and looked up at a long double-barreled shotgun in the hands of a Texian. "Yo dude, I surrender! I surrender!" Nick spouted.

The other man aimed a pistol at Nick. "Hold up, Deaf. He's only a boy!" the man with the deep voice exclaimed.

"How can you tell with all that mud on him?" The man called Deaf inserted his shotgun into a scabbard. He slid off his horse and grabbed Nick by the back of his jacket, yanking him up to his feet. Deaf's wavy brown hair was dirty and matted beneath a rumpled hat. He hadn't shaved in days, and the glare in his piercing green eyes held nei-ther fear nor compassion.

"Take it easy, mister," Nick pleaded as Deaf shook him. The man withdrew a long knife from his belt.

"He's a boy, Deaf!" Hendrick shouted.

Keeping an eye on the knife, Nick struggled to loosen his jacket from the man's grip. "Listen to what he's saying! I'm just a kid!"

Deaf slowly lowered his knife. "That ain't Spanish

you're talking. Who are you?"

"Nick Taylor."

Deaf pulled Nick closer. The man's sunburned face seemed to grow redder. "What the blazes are you doing in that Mexican uniform, Nick Taylor? You don't sound much like a *soldado.*"

"I'm not a *soldado.* They made me wear it," Nick mumbled.

"Come again. You have to speak up," Deaf snapped.

"I said they made me wear it," Nick shouted at the man.

Hendrick shoved his pistol into his belt and dismounted. He picked up the hat from the ground and handed it to Nick. "Let the boy go, Deaf."

Deaf? Nick thought back to a school project he had worked on last year. "Are you Deaf Smith? The same Deaf Smith who burned down Vince's Bridge?"

"How'd you know that, being it just happened yesterday?" Hendrick demanded.

"I hear people talking . . ." Nick's voice faded as he looked up at Hendrick. The man was very tall. Shadows fell on his face from his wide-brimmed hat. He had curly black hair. "Who are you?" Nick asked.

"He's Hendrick Arnold," Deaf said. "Besides being my son-in-law, Hendrick is one fine spy. We're desperate men, boy. Best not forget it."

Journey to San Jacinto

"Somethin' ain't right 'bout him, Deaf," Hendrick muttered, taking a step closer to Nick. "He knows too much."

Deaf shook Nick again. "What's your business here?"

Frustrated, Nick jerked himself loose. "You want the truth? Here it is. I'm from the future. I read about both of you in a history book. That's how I know things, and I know a lot of things."

Hendrick chuckled. "Got plenty of lip for a priz'ner."

Nick glanced down at the hat clenched in his hands. He put a finger through a hole near the top and held it up. "Do you see this? You guys almost shot me."

"What's all the fuss about?" Deaf growled. "You're alive, ain't you?"

"That's not the point," Nick argued.

Hendrick stared at Nick. "What we gonna do with this young pup?" Nick took a big step back.

Deaf grabbed Nick's arm again and cracked a smile. Tobacco juice stained his lower teeth. "We could shoot him for back-talking us, Hendrick. Just take a moment to reload my shotgun."

"Hey," Nick complained, "I'm an American. I know my rights. My aunt is a lawyer."

"Plenty of backbone too," Hendrick scoffed. "Still waitin' to hear how ya wound up in that uniform."

Musket shots rang out. Both men turned toward the

battlefield. Deaf frowned. "We'll have to deal with him later."

Hendrick nodded. "Best drop him off in those trees, back behind the Texian line. The battle's still fresh. Give ever'one a chance to cool down and think straight. Give us time to finish what we come here for."

Deaf dragged Nick over to his horse and grasped the saddle horn. He released Nick and pulled himself up into the saddle. "You ride with me, boy."

Nick gazed back at Cesar in the group of horses. "Can I ride the black one over there? He knows me."

"Be quick about it," Hendrick said as he mounted his horse. "Don't even think about ridin' another direction."

"Whatever," Nick exhaled. He put his fingers to his mouth and whistled. Cesar's ears perked up. Nick jogged toward the horses. He slowed down as he reached Cesar. "It's only me," Nick said gently. He held out his hand and let the horse sniff it. Nick seized the loose reins, pulled himself up into the saddle, and trotted over to Deaf and Hendrick. With Nick in the middle, they headed toward the Texian line.

CHAPTER FOURTEEN

⇥⇤

Reunion

Jackie paced around to the front of the wagon where the horses once stood. The Texian cavalry had taken James's horses away earlier that afternoon. "Stupid trunk," she muttered. "Why couldn't this be a peaceful time period?"

Hannah sat on the wagon seat and watched Jackie complete another lap. A single musket fired loudly.

Jackie flinched. "I hate that sound!"

"The battle's supposed to be over, and they're only rounding up prisoners now," Hannah said. "Miss Barrington should be back soon. Captain Seguín wanted us—"

"Hide, Hannah!" Jackie hissed, scrambling up into the wagon. "I just saw a Mexican soldier."

Hannah quickly pulled the canvas cover closed in the

115

front of the wagon and then in the back. A small opening remained in the center where the canvas edges didn't meet. She peeked out of the hole. A muddy Mexican soldier was riding through the trees on a black horse. He was headed their way!

Jackie grabbed Hannah's arm and pulled her to the front corner of the wagon. "Stay down or he'll see you," Jackie whispered. The girls exchanged nervous glances and held their breath.

Something scratched against the outside of the canvas cover. Jackie's eyes widened as the scratching sound came closer to where they were sitting. Hannah put her finger to her lips, gesturing for Jackie to remain silent.

A horse whinnied. Grass swished as someone stomped along the outside of the wagon. Something splashed in the water barrel—the soldier was getting a drink.

They heard footsteps again as the soldier climbed up into the front of the wagon. One dirty hand reached into the small canvas opening, grasping at the edges.

"Agh!" Jackie screamed. Hannah's heart pounded. Both girls scurried to the back of the wagon. They huddled together.

A grizzled voice growled, "Put yer hands up high where I can see 'em and turn 'round."

"Is that James?" Hannah whispered.

Jackie nodded.

"Now climb down from there nice and slow," the man

ordered. "Don't try anything cuz I'd be obliged to shoot ya. You gals all right in thar?"

"James, is that you?" Hannah shouted.

"I'm here, missy, but I ain't alone. I jest captured me a priz'ner."

"Be careful, James," Jackie warned. "That Mexican soldier looked mean."

"You're right about the mean part," a familiar voice grumbled. "It's payback time . . . ouch!"

Hannah's eyebrows drew together. "That sounds—"

"—like Nick," Jackie said.

Hannah quickly loosened the canvas ties. They peered out of the wagon. There was Nick in a Mexican uniform. Splotches of dirt covered most of his face and uniform. Gooey mud clung to his pants below the knees. James stood behind Nick, his rifle aimed in Nick's direction.

Nick glared at Hannah. "Who is this guy?" he shouted. James poked Nick sharply in the ribs with his rifle. "Hey, watch it!" Nick hollered, pushing the rifle aside. "Don't you know anything about gun safety?"

Jackie's mouth dropped open. "James, that's no Mexican soldier. That's Hannah's brother!"

"Yer Hannah's brother?" James bellowed. "Why in the world are ya dressed like that, boy? Ya don't seem to have the sense God gave a prairie dog. I could of shot ya."

The two girls quickly climbed out of the wagon. Hannah ran to Nick and threw her arms around him in a giant hug. Nick glowered and pushed her away.

"Aren't you glad to see me?"

Nick clenched his fists. "I told you not to mess around with that trunk again!"

Jackie jumped in front of Hannah. "She's been worried sick about you."

"Shut up, Jackie," Nick snapped. "This is between me and Hannah."

James prodded Nick with the rifle barrel again. "That ain't no way to talk to those young gals."

"Those young gals," Nick drawled, trying to imitate James's accent, "almost got me killed."

Everyone was shouting at once. Hannah and Jackie were upset at Nick for trying to scare them. James was trying to find out why Nick was dressed like the enemy, and Nick was letting the girls know exactly what he thought of them.

BANG! Hannah spun around. Captain Seguín was sitting on his horse, holding a pistol pointed at the sky. A puff of smoke spread out, filling the air with the bitter smell of gunpowder.

"What's going on?" Miss Barrington asked as she and Private Cruz guided their horses closer. She stared down at Nick. "And who are you?"

Answers exploded from all directions, but James's voice overpowered the others. "This here boy is Hannah's brother. Seems he saw Santa Anna headin' west on horse-back."

"That is extremely important information," Miss Barrington said. *"Santa Anna se dirije hacia el oeste a caballo."*

Private Cruz nodded. *"Yo lo perseguiré."* He galloped off in the direction James had directed.

Hannah gently tapped Nick's shoulder. "That lady is Miss Barrington, Mr. Barrington's niece," she said.

"Just what we need, another Barrington," Nick remarked with a sour expression.

"Yo necesito hablar con el muchacho," Captain Seguín said. He dismounted and took Nick by the arm. Nick pulled away from him.

Miss Barrington eased herself off the horse. "I'll interpret for you, Nick. Captain Seguín just wants to ask you a few questions."

"Why should I tell him anything?" Nick scoffed.

Captain Seguín said, *"Me vas a decir lo que sabes o te voy a tomar como prisionero."*

Miss Barrington explained, "If you don't cooperate, Captain Seguín will take you in as a prisoner."

Nick rolled his eyes. "Can this day get any better?" He followed Seguín and Miss Barrington away from the group. Hannah watched her brother while James chatted with Jackie. Nick looked like he was angry at the world.

"They have Houston in the shade of an oak tree," James said. "The doc's tendin' to him. A musket ball struck his ankle. Lost his favorite horse, Saracen, too."

"How sad," Jackie said.

"Shot right out from under him, and that wasn't the half of it. Each time he lost a horse, they brung him another." James prattled on until Captain Seguín walked back to the group. Nick lingered by the black horse.

"Señorita Barrington," Captain Seguín said, *"si cabalgamos ahorita, tal vez encontraremos a su tío antes de oscurecer."*

"He says if we ride out now, we might find my uncle before it gets dark," Miss Barrington explained. James helped her back on her horse.

Nick approached Miss Barrington. "Would you ask him if I can go along?" he asked. "I need to find some friends."

Miss Barrington translated, *"Nick quiere venir. El busca a alguien."*

Captain Seguín crossed his arms and studied Nick's face and then his uniform. *"Lo voy a permitir mientras permanezca junto a mi."*

"As long as you stay close, Nick," Miss Barrington said.

Nick nodded. "Two Texians already got in my face with that 'bring 'em back dead or alive' attitude. I had to convince them that I wasn't the enemy."

"Thank goodness," Miss Barrington said.

"Nothing good about it," Nick mumbled. "Nothing good about anything that happened today."

CHAPTER FIFTEEN

The Survivors

Captain Seguín, Miss Barrington, and Nick rode their horses down the gentle slope to the battlefield. Not a word was spoken as they entered a world ruled by war. Bloody bodies littered the field, and they rode from one to another looking for signs of Mr. Barrington. Nick hoped he wouldn't see anyone familiar among the fallen.

"Oh my," Miss Barrington gasped as she covered her mouth with her hand. There was an unnatural stillness over the land, broken by cries of pain from the injured and dying men. The air had a thickness to it as if spirits surrounded the living, trying to hold on while death lingered, patient now, and waited for what couldn't be stopped.

Texian and Mexican soldiers tended their wounded comrades scattered across the land. A somber expression covered the faces of the men they passed. Hundreds of Mexican soldiers had lost their lives.

Farther down in the prairie, Nick spotted the Mexicans' brass cannon. Behind it, a lone *soldado* kneeled in the grass, his head bent down. Nick nudged Cesar's flanks and trotted toward the man. Beside the soldier was the lifeless body of General Castrillón. His courage and dedication to duty had cost him his life. Nick tried to look away, but couldn't.

The *soldado* glanced up at the riders. It was Miguel! The once-proud warrior was covered in dirt and smoke. Blood seeped through the shoulder of his uniform. An unbelieving expression on his pale face told a story that needed no words; he was grieving.

"Miss Barrington," Nick said, his voice just above a whisper, "that guy's name is Miguel. The man that he's kneeling by is . . ." Nick choked on his words. He remembered when General Castrillón had called him down from the tree. The soldiers below had had a good laugh at his expense until the general ordered them away. Then he thought about that morning, when General Castrillón killed the snake, and how Diego picked it up and ran with it, weaving through the men as they cheered him on. General Castrillón had even offered him a home in

Mexico. Why did he have to die? And where was Diego?

Nick slid off the horse and stood beside Miguel. During the battle, Miguel had forced him to take cover. Now it was time to return the favor. Nick stammered, "The man there . . . on the ground . . . is General Castrillón. Miguel is his aide. They're . . . they're the reason I'm still alive."

Miss Barrington and Captain Seguín quickly dismounted to assist Miguel. She tore off a ruffle from her petticoat. Miguel sat unmoving, but didn't resist as she and Captain Seguín removed his jacket and opened up his shirt. They bandaged up the wound as best they could. While they helped him put his jacket back on, Seguín spoke quietly to Miguel in Spanish.

Miss Barrington said, "I think he'll be all right. The wound isn't too severe. And Captain Seguín promised Miguel that General Castrillón will receive a proper burial. A man who lives near here by the name of Zavala was well acquainted with the general."

Nick stared at the ground. "I should have done something."

Miss Barrington touched his arm. "You couldn't have prevented it. This is what happens in history."

Nick walked over to Cesar. He watched Captain Seguín, out of respect for a fallen enemy, pull a blanket from his saddlebag and cover the general's body with it.

Moisture stung Nick's eyes. He rubbed Cesar's head one more time before he grasped the reins, leading him back to Miguel. "Here, Miguel. He's yours now," Nick said.

"*Gracias, Nicholas*," Miguel said, rising to his feet.

Nick glanced at Miss Barrington. "Would you ask Miguel what happened to my friend, Diego?"

Miss Barrington translated the question, but Nick barely heard the response. From the expression on Miguel's face, Nick knew that Diego hadn't survived.

Miss Barrington's eyes filled with sympathetic tears. "I'm sorry, Nick. Most of their unit perished. Try to remember Diego as you last saw him."

Nick held Cesar's reins as Miguel struggled to pull himself up onto Cesar's back. The horse restlessly pawed the ground. Nick leaned his head against Cesar's neck. "I know how you feel, boy."

Nodding politely to Miss Barrington, Captain Seguín said, "*Yo los acompañaré al campo y luego atenderé al prisionero.*"

Miss Barrington patted Nick's shoulder. "Captain Seguín will escort us back to camp before he takes Miguel to where they're holding the prisoners. You can ride double with me."

Nick took in a deep breath and held it for a moment. History was nothing like the words printed in books. It could be harsh, unfeeling. Those written words scratched only the surface of the story. The details lurking underneath, hidden and sometimes purposefully forgotten, were how it actually played out. He had seen both sides of the Texas Revolution, and it was nothing like he could have imagined.

"Let's go, Nick," Miss Barrington encouraged.

Nick cocked his head to the side. "Wait, I hear something." He remained completely still. "There it is again." He waded through the grass, searching for the source of the sound. Miss Barrington followed him, leading her horse by the reins.

"Help," a weak voice called out. This time the voice was louder.

All at once, a cry erupted from Miss Barrington. "Uncle David!" She released the horse's reins and dropped to the ground as Nick and Captain Seguín rushed over to her. Hidden by the tall grass was Mr. Barrington. He lay motionless while Miss Barrington held his hand. Tears spilled from her eyes.

Mr. Barrington looked different from the last time Nick had seen him. He had grown a beard. Instead of his suit and tie, he wore plain clothes, like the other Texians who worked the land for a living. His hair was matted with blood on one side of his head, and a bump was starting to swell. His left arm was bent back in an unusual position.

"Uncle David, can you hear me?" Miss Barrington asked. She gently touched his cheek.

Mr. Barrington's eyes cracked open at the sound of her voice. "Georgia, is that you?" he whispered hoarsely.

Miguel rode Cesar closer and studied Mr. Barrington's face. Miss Barrington tore another ruffle from her petticoat as Miguel muttered something in Spanish to her. Captain Seguín helped Mr. Barrington up to a sitting position and gave him a drink of water from a gourd.

Miss Barrington said, "Miguel saw him toward the end of the battle. Uncle David was trying to assist a wounded soldier. Miguel's not sure what happened after that."

"Where am I?" Mr. Barrington asked as his niece wrapped his arm snugly against his body.

"You're at the San Jacinto battleground, Uncle David. You've been injured. Do you think you can ride a horse?"

Mr. Barrington's eyelids fluttered, closed, and reopened. He drew in a ragged breath and reached up to the others.

Nick and Captain Seguín helped Mr. Barrington to his feet while Miss Barrington led Captain Seguín's horse over to them. They boosted Mr. Barrington up on the horse. He slumped over as he clung to the saddle horn. Taking the reins, Captain Seguín walked along, leading the horse at a slow pace.

Miss Barrington looked worried. "Hurry, Nick. He needs a doctor." As Nick got on the horse behind Miss Barrington, she asked, "How do we get home?"

"Something has to trigger it," Nick explained. "When we went back in time to the Battle of the Alamo, I was holding a little model of the Alamo. After I opened its front doors, we traveled to the past. That same thing sent us ahead again to our present time. You, Hannah, or Jackie must have touched or opened something from the trunk."

"We examined several artifacts," Miss Barrington said.

"Whatever it was," Nick said, "your uncle should know. The sooner we're away from here, the better."

CHAPTER SIXTEEN

⇥⇤

The Prisoner

Hannah held her breath as Miss Barrington and Nick rode toward the campsite. Behind them, Captain Seguín led the horse carrying Mr. Barrington. On a black horse was another man whom Hannah didn't recognize.

"They found Mr. B!" Jackie exclaimed as she tugged at Hannah's arm. The girls raced ahead to meet the riders.

The horses moved slowly. Mr. Barrington grimaced as the horse swayed with each step. "Mr. Barrington, are you okay?" Hannah asked.

Her teacher looked bewildered. "I believe so," he answered weakly.

"He's been injured," Miss Barrington said. "You were right all along, Hannah."

"I knew he needed our help," Hannah declared with a smile. "If we hadn't come here—" Hannah swallowed her words as she noticed Nick's dismal expression.

Jackie hurried toward Captain Seguín's horse and looked up at her teacher. "Mr. B, what happened out there?" she asked.

Mr. Barrington focused on Jackie. He mumbled, "Do I know you?"

Astounded, Jackie followed her teacher until Captain Seguín stopped the horse near the wagon. "How could you forget me? I'm Jackie, one of your best students!"

"Your voice sounds familiar," Mr. Barrington said, "but I don't recall your face."

"But . . . but, I have an unforgettable face," Jackie gasped.

As Nick and Miss Barrington dismounted, James helped Mr. Barrington off the horse and into the wagon. Miss Barrington and Jackie followed them inside. "I sit in the last row of your classroom," Jackie babbled, "you know, by the window."

Captain Seguín pulled himself up on his horse, close to Miguel. The captain touched the side of his hat. *"Adiós, Hannah."*

"Miguel," Nick said, as he held out his hand. *"Gracias."*

Miguel shook his hand. *"Buena suerte, Nicholas,"* Miguel said. *"Que bueno que encontraste a tus amigos."* The men turned their horses and rode away from the camp.

Nick slid his hands into his pockets and walked back to the wagon. His eyes met Hannah's as if he wanted to say something. Instead, he sat down on the ground, slumping against the spokes of the wagon wheel. Hannah knelt down beside him. "What did Miguel say to you?"

Nick stared toward the battlefield. "Something about wishing me luck. I'm not sure what the rest was."

Reaching out, Hannah touched his arm. Nick tensed up. "Are you okay?" she asked.

Nick's eyes were as dark as the ocean. "I'm here, aren't I?" he mumbled.

"What's that mean?"

"I saw things—stuff kids shouldn't see."

"It's my fault," Hannah said. Her head hung down. "I didn't think anything bad would happen."

Tapping his feet against the ground, Nick knocked clumps of dried mud from his boots. He looked up as Jackie clambered down from the wagon. "What happened to you, Jackie?" Nick asked. "You're a mess."

As Jackie attempted to straighten out her tangled hair, she glared at Nick. "I can't help how I look. Besides, you're a hundred times dirtier than me."

"Jackie," Hannah said firmly, "Nick's been through a lot."

"Just look at him, Hannah." Jackie shook an accusing

finger at Nick. "He's playing you. He wants you to feel sorry for him."

"The Mexican army is vicious and hates North Americans," Nick taunted. He scratched at the dried mud on his cheek. "They were getting ready to torture me."

Jackie marched toward him. "I'm sure they make all North Americans change into their uniforms just before they start poking them with lances."

Hannah stared at Nick. He probably was stretching the truth, but there was something else in his eyes, something dreadful.

"Girls," Miss Barrington interrupted as she climbed out of the wagon. James was right behind her. "My uncle received a hard blow on his head, and he's apparently lost some of his memory. He has no idea where he is or where his trunk might be."

"Oh, no," Jackie moaned.

"Could be packed away in one of the wagons 'round here," James said.

Nick rose to his feet. "Let's start looking."

"Listen, boy," James said. "You ain't goin' nowhere dressed like that."

Nick shrugged. "It's all I have."

"There's some clothes in the back of my wagon that jest might fit."

Nick jumped into the wagon and was back in a matter of minutes. He stood before them like a true Texas pioneer, in loose pants with patches and a homespun shirt. He pulled his gray hat down tightly on his head and asked, "Where do we start?"

CHAPTER SEVENTEEN

Search for the Trunk

"I'm going with you," Hannah insisted.

"Oh no you're not," Nick spouted from atop Miss Barrington's horse.

"Oh yes I am," Hannah said. She approached James on his horse. "I know what the trunk looks like. We'll find it faster together."

"Count me in," Jackie added.

"No way," Nick groaned.

There was a spark of determination in Hannah's eyes. "I'm going along if I have to walk."

James scratched at the whiskers on his chin. He looked sympathetically at Hannah. "Go ahead an' ride with yer brother."

Hannah beamed as she approached Nick on the horse. Nick pulled back on the reins, leading the horse away from her.

"Nick!" Hannah snapped.

James removed a small tin from a pocket on his shirt. He opened it up, took out a pinch of tobacco, and placed it between his lower lip and teeth. It made a bump on the outside of his chin. "Let her up thar, boy," he barked. "I won't tell ya agin."

"Whatever," Nick mumbled. Without another word, he lowered his arm to help Hannah up on the back of his horse.

Jackie gathered her long skirt in her hands and rushed over to James. "I'll ride with you, James."

"Miss Barrington needs yer help keepin' an eye on her uncle, missy," James said softly. "Best stay here. Wouldn't want any cougars chasin' us." He winked at Jackie.

"Ha ha, very funny, James." Jackie pouted as she looked back at the wagon.

"Now mind what I say," James cautioned gently. He turned his horse and rode away from the camp. Hannah and Nick followed.

James squinted suspiciously at Nick as the horses loped side by side. "I reckon it's time ya told me how ya ended up with the Mexican army, boy."

"Hannah and I were separated by accident. While I was

looking for her, the Mexican army marched up. I hid in a tree, but they found me."

James spat out a stream of tobacco juice. "Yer mighty lucky to be alive."

Nick shook his head. "It wasn't like that. Their general sort of looked out for me. He was a good man."

"Humph," James grunted. He wiped the tobacco remains from his mouth on his sleeve. "Why ya reckon that trunk is so dadgum important?"

"It belongs to Mr. Barrington," Hannah replied. "He won't leave here without it."

James began to whistle as they rode through the trees until they came upon several unattended wagons that belonged to the Texian army. Hannah and Nick searched carefully through each one, disappointment growing on their faces. The trunk wasn't in any of the wagons.

They rode on until they heard voices. A group of men were standing under a shady oak tree. "Look, Hannah," Nick said. He stopped the horse. "That's Houston on the ground. It's just like the famous painting in all the Texas history books."

Houston sat with his back against the tree. A white strip of material was wrapped around his ankle and halfway up his leg. The Texians were gathered around him with concerned expressions. "The only one missing is Santa Anna," Nick muttered.

"Where's he?"

Nick shrugged as he urged the horse forward.

"Where are we going?" Hannah whispered anxiously.

James trotted up on his horse and yanked the reins from Nick's hands. Nick looked the man square in the eyes. "Let me go, James."

"What's on yer mind, boy?" James said sternly.

Nick kept his focus on Houston. "A friend of mine died here today. Diego was only a kid, a drummer for the Mexican army. Houston should know about that."

A friend died? Hannah thought uneasily.

James twisted the reins around his hand in a firm grip. "Houston seen what happened out thar. And he ain't gonna wanna hear about how ya marched in with the Mexican army."

"But it's not fair," Nick muttered. He continued to stare at Houston.

James pulled the reins in tighter, moving their horses closer. "I know yer angry, son," James said. His voice lost its harsh edge. "We're all angry. It'll only pass with time. We all remember what happened at the Alamo and Goliad. Hundreds of men . . . our friends and brothers, were slaughtered. We have the future to tend to now. We paid dearly fer our freedom . . . so did the Mexicans. Houston can't bring yer friend back."

"James is right," Hannah agreed. "Let's keep going, Nick."

Nick exhaled in disgust and tugged at the reins until James released them. They traveled on until they came upon three more wagons. A man stood beside the closest wagon. He was an average height but thin and wiry; a tight belt around his waist held his baggy clothes in place. A large snare drum lay at his feet. He lifted up a canteen and took a drink.

"Looks like someone's slave over yonder," James said.

"Slave," Hannah muttered. "You don't own slaves, do you, James?"

James shook his head. "All my worldly goods are tied up in my rig and horses."

"Let's ask him if he's seen the trunk," Nick suggested.

"Howdy," James announced as they neared the man.

"Howdy." The man removed a dust-covered floppy hat and wiped his face with a blue bandana. There was a weary look in his deep brown eyes. On the ground beside his feet, a silver sword shone through the tall blades of grass.

"We're lookin' fer a missin' trunk," James said.

The man nodded. "Could be anywhere 'round here."

"May we check through these wagons?" Hannah asked shyly.

"Don't mind me." The man took another long drink from the canteen. "Hope it ain't in that one over yonder." One wagon sat apart from the others. There was only one wheel still standing upright. A ripped cloth cover was collapsed in the middle of the wagon bed, and the back half was smashed. Splinters of wood littered the ground.

"Looks like that one took some cannon shot," James commented.

Nick quickly got off the horse and then helped Hannah dismount. He climbed into the first wagon while James sat patiently on his horse. Hannah walked toward the man. "I'm Hannah and this is James. That's my brother in the wagon."

"Pleased to meet you, Hannah and James. I'm Dick," the man said.

"Is that your drum?" Hannah asked.

"It is," Dick replied, "and I played it while we marched into battle."

Hannah took another step forward. She folded her hands behind her back. "Can I see your sword?"

James cleared his throat and gave Hannah a vexed look.

Dick bent down to pick up the sword. He handed it to Hannah. "It's sharp," he cautioned.

Hannah held the heavy sword in her open hands. Its handle was brass, and there were etched curlicue designs on the blade near the hilt.

"Mighty fancy sword fer a drummer," James muttered.

Dick chuckled. "Found it out on the battlefield. S'pose it belonged to a Mexican officer."

Hannah gave the sword back to the man. "May I ask you a personal question?"

Journey to San Jacinto

Dick nodded. "Go on ahead."

"Are you a slave?" Hannah surprised both James and herself at her boldness.

Dick shook his head. "Proud to say I'm a free man. There are a few slaves here, though."

"Why did you join the army?" Hannah asked.

"They promised me land if I'd muster up." Dick said with a slight smile. He looked off into the distance. "I barely make a livin' as a tinker, fixin' things for folks, but ownin' my own land . . ."

Hannah thought about what Dick had said as she watched Nick walk slowly toward the broken wagon.

"Might as well go ahead, boy," James hollered. "If it's in thar . . . I'd rather wrestle a bear than fetch back a busted-up trunk. Miss Barrington'll most likely blame both armies if that trunk's been blown to smithereens."

A soft breath of cold wind blew against the back of Hannah's neck like an omen. She shivered. "Wait for me, Nick."

Dick set the sword down. "Maybe I best help them."

Nick and Hannah tugged at one side of the canvas cover. Dick grabbed the other side. The cover ripped, tearing down the middle. Nick pulled the canvas back until it opened up to reveal a catastrophe within. Broken, charred, and shattered boxes were everywhere.

Hannah felt that cold breath of air on the back of her neck again. Clenching her skirt, she climbed into what was left of the wagon bed. Nick leaned over the edge of the wagon and threw out pieces of wood. They dug to the bottom together, debris flying everywhere, and then they stopped.

"Oh, no!" Hannah gasped.

James rode up and peered over Dick's shoulder. Nick and Hannah gathered scraps of wood into a pile at the side of the wagon. "What's that, boy?" James asked.

Nick picked up a dark brown section of wood with hinges. "We found what's left of Mr. Barrington's trunk."

CHAPTER EIGHTEEN

The Missing Piece

It was dusk as Hannah and Nick finally made it back to camp. Nick dismounted and held the reins as Hannah got off the horse. The air was crisp and fresh. Chilled, Hannah rubbed her arms to warm them. Jackie and Miss Barrington helped Mr. Barrington down from the wagon.

James lagged behind, dragging the trunk—now just a bundle of wood and hinges—from a rope tied to his saddle. Pulling up on the reins, James brought his horse to a stop. He loosened the ropes from the saddle horn.

"Hannah, Mr. B finally remembers us," Jackie reported. She frowned as she watched James wind the rope in a loop around his arm. "No way! That can't be the trunk!"

Nick exhaled loudly. "It's not exactly the way you remember it."

Hannah closed her eyes. "We'll have to fix it somehow."

Everyone gathered around the trunk, now no more than large pieces of brown wood covered with spirals, zigzags, and arrows. There were no sounds of cymbals or bugle calls this time.

"I don't know why y'all are so worried 'bout these scraps of lumber," James grumbled. "Ain't like ya lost a loved one."

Mr. Barrington leaned on his niece for support. She asked, "Does any of this look familiar to you, Uncle David?"

"The design on the wood reminds me . . ." Mr. Barrington concentrated on the damaged trunk. Suddenly his face lit up. "I can match the pieces, but we need a carpenter." He knelt down and separated a jagged section from the pile. "Hannah's right. We have no choice but to reassemble it. We can't leave here without it."

"We met someone who wants to help us," Hannah explained. "His name is Dick. He knows how to fix things. He'll be here any minute."

"That's wonderful," Miss Barrington said. She helped her uncle spread out the sections of the trunk. "Uncle David, you should be careful with your injured arm."

Mr. Barrington shook his head. "I'll be fine, Georgia. Let's get started." With his good arm, he moved some sections to the side. He wavered, touched his head, and winced.

Hannah knelt down beside him. "Mr. Barrington, why don't you let us sort through the pieces, and you can tell us which piece belongs to what side?"

"Why, of course!" Miss Barrington agreed. "Uncle David, you are only to supervise. James, please start a large fire so we'll have some light to work by. Girls, let's get started."

"It's almost like a jigsaw puzzle," Jackie said. "I'm good at puzzles." As Mr. Barrington gave them directions, they shifted the pieces around.

James grunted as he removed the saddle from his horse and set it on the ground. "Why can't y'all jest wait fer mornin' light?"

"Please," Jackie said sweetly. "It's getting hard to see."

"All right," James growled. "I'll start yer fire. You womenfolk never give me a spare moment."

"Tell me about it, dude," Nick responded.

"Come on, boy, you can help me with the fire," James muttered. "Did ya hear a *thank you, James, for findin' our trunk?* Maybe it was better ya came with the Mexican army."

By the time James and Nick had a fire going, the sections of the trunk had been categorized by sides, bottom, and top. It appeared that nothing was missing except someone to assemble it.

Reaching into his wagon, James lifted up his cauldron and set it on the ground. Next, he removed a large cloth bag and rummaged through it. "Would one of y'all fetch me 'nough water from the barrel to fill up this here kettle? We'll all be hungry as wolves come mornin'."

Jackie agreed as James carried the cauldron to the fire. She dipped a pail into the water barrel and handed it to James. After pouring the water into the cauldron, he added several handfuls of dried beans and seasoning. Humming contentedly to himself, he stirred the contents with a long-handled spoon.

The bushes rustled as Dick rode into camp. "How-do, folks. Where's the trunk?" Miss Barrington helped her uncle to his feet as Dick dismounted from his horse. Everyone gathered near the trunk.

"Hmmm," Dick muttered, stooping down beside the splintered wood. He picked up a piece and examined it.

"Can you put it back together?" Hannah asked.

"I'll try my best, Hannah," Dick said. He walked back to his horse and removed a leather pouch and a wooden hammer from a saddlebag.

"Maybe I can help him," James mumbled. "It'll be hours before the food is ready."

Hannah, Nick, and Jackie sat down on the ground on

Journey to San Jacinto

the opposite side of the campfire from the men assembling the trunk. It had been a long day for all of them. Hannah stared into the golden flames. *What if they can't fix the trunk?* she thought.

Jackie pushed her sleeve up and held her arm toward Nick. "Here's where I was attacked by the cougar," she announced excitedly. Dark scabs had formed over the claw marks. "How am I gonna explain this to my mom?"

Nick leaned toward Jackie and looked at her arm. "Does it hurt?" he asked.

Jackie straightened out her sleeve. "Only a little. How about you? Did you see the battle?"

Nick nodded. "Way too much."

Mr. Barrington took his niece's arm and approached the kids. "How did you get here?" he asked softly enough so James and Dick wouldn't overhear.

"We were going through your trunk," Hannah said.

"And suddenly it was 1836," Miss Barrington added. "It was simply amazing. Nick said we must have triggered something. How do we get home, Uncle David?"

"I still can't remember," Mr. Barrington admitted. "Everything jumbles together in my mind. I don't recall crossing Buffalo Bayou or the battle itself. I sincerely apologize, Georgia."

"Wait a minute, Miss B," Jackie interrupted. The light from the fire reflected on her animated face. "Just before we went back in time, you were looking at something."

"That's right," Hannah agreed. "I was trying on those huge gloves you called gauntlets . . . and you found something with initials on it. What was it?"

Miss Barrington looked thoughtful. Then her eyes opened wide. "Yes, I remember. It was a gold pocket watch with two letters engraved on the front. One letter was worn away, almost impossible to distinguish. The other, I believe, was an *H.*"

"Houston," Hannah and Jackie said in unison.

"I opened it," Miss Barrington recalled, "and there was engraving inside."

"Where's the watch?" Nick asked.

"Funny, I'd forgotten all about it until now." As she slipped her left hand into the folds of her dress, Miss Barrington smiled. She removed a shiny gold object attached to a chain. It was the watch she had found in the classroom. "Isn't this a lovely piece?"

Jackie rolled her eyes in disgust. "Open that thing so we can get out of here."

"Wait," Mr. Barrington warned. "We need the trunk in place first. Then, and only then, do we dare open the watch."

"What about James and Dick?" Nick asked.

"They need to be as far away as possible. We don't want any witnesses," Mr. Barrington said.

CHAPTER NINETEEN

The Ring

Using rags as a potholder, Hannah lifted the lid on the cauldron and stirred the simmering contents. A delicious aroma filled the air. It had been almost a day since anyone had eaten, and she was starving.

A wolf howled nearby. Startled, Hannah banged the hot lid down on the cauldron. Her skin prickled as she glanced anxiously around. She had spent a restless night listening to nature's voices. Shadows beyond the camp teased her imagination.

Although it was morning, the sun hadn't reached the horizon. James was asleep on a bedroll beside the wagon. He snored loudly. Miss Barrington was caring for her uncle inside the wagon, and Jackie was dozing beside the fire. The wolf howled again. Where was Nick?

Hannah walked over to the trunk, which was now in two parts. The top lay on the ground, tightly knotted ropes binding it together. The bottom half was in better shape. Wooden pins were stuck through the edges and corners to hold it in place. An air of mystery still surrounded the trunk, but was it enough to get them back to their time?

"Ready to go?" Nick called out unexpectedly. Hannah turned around as he sauntered through the trees, his eyes hidden by the brim of his hat.

"That howling wolf is so creepy," Hannah shivered. "Where were you?"

"I hiked back down to the battlefield." His voice trailed off. "A lot happened out there."

"It must have been a nightmare," Hannah murmured. Her heart ached for her brother.

"When I was down there just now, I saw some Texians walking along with a prisoner. It was Santa Anna. I wanted to make sure we didn't mess up the timeline and allow him to escape. He doesn't deserve an easy way out."

Hannah looked curiously at Nick. "Who was Diego?"

"Later, Hannah. Help me drag the trunk away from the camp. We need to make sure James doesn't see us leave."

Jackie stood up and stretched. "James is knocked out. I'll take the top." The three of them moved the trunk several yards away and hid it behind some trees and bushes. Then Hannah hurried back to the wagon. She tiptoed past James. "Miss Barrington, we're ready to go home," she hissed into the wagon's opening.

Miss Barrington crept out of the wagon. Together, the two of them helped Mr. Barrington down. His face wasn't as pale as before, but he moaned as he bumped his arm against the side of the canvas cover. Silently, they joined Nick and Jackie.

Nick carefully set the top on the trunk. Everyone gathered in a circle. "We're all in place," Mr. Barrington said. He pointed at Hannah. "You may open it now, young lady."

Hannah touched the top of the trunk and smiled. Nick helped her lift the lid, and they placed it on the ground. Mr. Barrington nodded to his niece. "The pocket watch is next," he directed.

Miss Barrington reached into her pocket and drew out the gold watch. The ancient timepiece sparkled in the early-morning light. She carefully pressed down on a small button at the side, releasing the cover.

"Aah!" Jackie exhaled. "On the inside it says 'To Sam with all my love.'"

Hannah felt something tighten on her finger. She held her hand up and looked at the ring she had purchased at the mall. The symbols were starting to revolve around the silver band.

Nick grabbed her arm and said something, but his voice buzzed past her like swarming bees. Hannah blinked, trying hard to concentrate. From somewhere behind her, a bugle call played softly. Nick shook Hannah's arm to get her attention as the bugle call grew louder. Mr. Barrington, Miss Barrington, and Jackie started to move in slow motion.

With a whoosh, a funnel of smoke swirled out of the trunk, surrounding everyone in its path. Hannah blinked again. Everyone was gone but Nick. They were still at the San Jacinto battleground!

CHAPTER TWENTY

One Final Surprise

"Why are we still here?" Nick demanded as he released Hannah's arm.

"I'm not sure," Hannah mumbled, "but look at the trunk." It was a shadow, merely particles of color suspended in air.

Curious, Nick reached out and passed his hand though its middle. It had no substance. "It feels cold."

Hannah stared at her hand. The ring tightened as the pattern turned slowly around the band.

Nick walked through the side of the trunk and stood in the middle. "It's like a freezer for ghosts. What's with the face, Hannah?"

She frowned. "It's this ring I'm wearing. It won't come off, and it's starting to hurt." Hannah's knuckle reddened as she tugged at the ring. "Maybe it's the reason we're still here. You were holding my arm when everyone else disappeared."

"What now?" Nick grumbled. He stepped through the back of the trunk. Hannah held out her hand so Nick could see the ring. "Whoa, the designs are moving," he said. "Where'd you get that?"

"At the mall, on Sunday."

"The designs look like the patterns on the trunk. That's why you bought it, isn't it?"

"Maybe." Hannah felt the ring tighten more.

Nick looked at her with suspicion. "What is it with you and this trunk? Even that ring is connected to it."

"Maybe Mr. Barrington can explain." Hannah pulled on the ring, but it wouldn't budge.

"We're getting out of here, Hannah, and that ring's gotta go." Nick impatiently grabbed her hand and spat on her finger.

"Gross! That's worse than the pain."

Nick smiled confidently at his sister. His eyes twinkled for the first time since they had been reunited. "Are you ready, Hannah?"

Hannah gritted her teeth and nodded. Nick twisted the ring.

"Oooowwww!" she cried. Hannah jerked her hand away from Nick.

"Do you want to stay here forever?" Nick exploded. "You did this, Hannah. You caused all of this to happen."

Hannah swallowed and took a deep breath. "I'm sorry."

Nick's face darkened. "Sorry doesn't cut it."

"You don't understand. Mr. Barrington needed our help, so—"

"Give me your hand, Hannah. I'll get that ring off."

Hannah crossed her arms and hid her hand beneath a sleeve. "Cold works on swelling, right?"

"So?"

"I have an idea." Hannah rushed back to the trunk with Nick right behind her. She bent down, eased her hand through the front of the trunk, and held it there. The pattern on the ring started to glow as it stopped spinning. "That feels better," Hannah said, wiggling her fingers. "Hey, it's starting to loosen up."

"Let's do it." With a firm grip on her hand, Nick forcefully wrenched the ring from her finger. He backed away, the ring clasped in his fist.

"Give it to me, Nick," Hannah pleaded. "It came from somewhere in Mexico."

"Then Mexico can have it back. It's time to go home, Hannah." With a smug look on his face, Nick hurled the ring through the trees.

"No!" Hannah shouted.

Bugle sounds blared. Trees blurred. The particles forming the trunk glimmered, and then POP! The trunk burst into shimmering swirls of light so bright that Hannah had to close her eyes.

"What took you so long?" Jackie sputtered. "I thought you were left behind for good."

Hannah opened her eyes and stared in amazement at the familiar classroom. Nick stood beside her. They both had on their school clothes.

"Thank goodness you're back," Miss Barrington said. Mr. Barrington smiled at Hannah.

"The trunk," Hannah murmured. "Look at it." There were a few more dents on the sides and top, but other than that, the trunk had somehow magically repaired itself. A smoky vapor floated above the trunk and a burnt smell lingered in the air. "What a trip," she whispered.

Nick's friend J.J. appeared in the doorway of the classroom. "Hey Nick, Coach wants to talk to us before school starts."

Jackie frowned. "You mean school hasn't even started?" she whined.

"Let's go, dude," J.J. insisted. "What's with the hat?"

Nick had an unreadable expression. He reached up and felt the gray hat he was still wearing—a hat that had survived the Battle of San Jacinto, just like he had. He smiled as he removed it. "Hang on to this for me, Hannah." Nick grasped the brim of the hat and tossed it across the room toward his sister. It glided gently into her hands.

Hannah bit her lip. She touched a small hole in the front of the hat. Her brows drew together as she inspected a matching hole in the back.

Nick picked up his backpack and headed to the door, where J.J. was waiting. "See you after school," Hannah said softly. She watched her brother and J.J. leave the room.

"Did you see the look he gave you?" Jackie bubbled. "He wants to tell you all about what happened with the Mexican army."

"Maybe," Hannah mumbled.

Suddenly a loud noise popped like a firecracker behind them. Everyone turned to gawk at a man they had never expected to see again. "What in tarnation?" James exclaimed. "Where's my horses and rig? Last thing I recall is this here ring flyin' smack-dab inta the side of my head."

He held out his hand and opened it. Nestled in his palm was Hannah's ring. "When I picked this up—" James glanced down at his clothes. "Well, I'll be."

"Oh, no!" Hannah and Jackie laughed together.

James stomped to the center of the group. He was dressed in blue jeans and a red plaid western shirt. A black cowboy hat was perched jauntily on his head. "I do like these fancy boots I'm wearin'. Some sort of snakeskin, looks like to me. Where'd they come from?"

Completely bewildered, Mr. Barrington sank down on a chair. "I'm not sure how to return him to the past."

Miss Barrington sighed loudly. "Uncle David, whatever will we do with him?"

"It looks like we have a houseguest, Georgia," Mr. Barrington replied.

Miss Barrington's mouth dropped open. "But—"

Jackie snickered and whispered to Hannah in an exaggerated Southern drawl, "I reckon Miss Georgia would've preferred to fetch back one of them han'some *Tejanos* 'stead of James."

Hannah giggled. "We warned her not to open that trunk!"

SPANISH TO ENGLISH TRANSLATION

(First time a word appears)

꒦꒷

CHAPTER 4

sombrero: *hat with a wide brim*

CHAPTER 5

adiós *goodbye*
norteamericano *North American*
¡Bájate de allí! *Come down from there!*
Más salsa, por favor. *More hot sauce, please.*
¿Qué haces aquí, muchacho? *What are you doing here, boy?*
soldados *soldiers*

CHAPTER 6

buenas tardes *good afternoon*
Mucho gusto, señor. *I'm pleased to meet you, sir.*

Con permiso, señoritas. *Excuse me, young ladies.*

Señor, yo soy Capitán Juan Seguín. *Sir, I am Captain Juan Seguín.*

Nosotros la encontraremos. *We will find her.*

Chapter 7

Tejas *Texas*

gracias *thank you*

¡No lo estás haciendo bien! *You're not doing it right!*

¡Oye, Montaño! ¿Qué pasó? *Hey, Montaño! What's happening?*

Deja enseñarte. *Let me show you.*

Chapter 8

Me da mucho gusto que te sientas mejor. *I'm glad you're feeling better.*

guisado *stew*

Chapter 9

¡Aquí te va! *Here it comes!*

¡Ay! ¿Qué fue eso? *Ouch! What was that?*

buenos dias *good morning*

Soy Diego. *I'm Diego.*

Chapter 10

¡Ándale! *Come on!*

otra vez *again*

CHAPTER 11

Aquí está, Nick. *Here, Nick.*

Es una cotimoth, dude. *It's a cottonmouth, dude.*

La víbora es tuya. *The snake is yours.*

Mira. *Look.*

¡Mira lo que tengo! *Look what I have!*

¿Quieres agua? *Do you want water?*

CHAPTER 12

Hay muchas víboras y animales cerca del pantano. *There are many snakes and other creatures near the bayou.*

CHAPTER 13

¡Correle, muchacho! ¡Hay vienen los norteamericanos! *Run, boy! The North Americans are coming!*

¡Fuego! *Fire!*

Me no Alamo, me no Goliad. *I didn't fight at the Alamo, I didn't fight at Goliad. (This is a direct quote based on eyewitness reports, but not a literal translation. The soldiers may have been trying to speak English.)*

¡Preparense! *Prepare yourselves!*

CHAPTER 14

Lo voy a permitir mientras permanezca junto a mi. *I will permit it as long as he remains close to me.*

Me vas a decir lo que sabes o te voy a tomar como
prisionero. *You will tell me what you know, or I will take you
in as a prisoner.*

Nick quiere venir. El busca a alguien. *Nick wants to come
along. He's looking for someone.*

Santa Anna se dirije hacia el oeste a caballo. *Santa Anna is
heading west on horseback.*

Yo lo perseguiré. *I'll go after him.*

Yo necesito hablar con el muchacho. *I need to talk to the boy.*

"Señorita Barrington," *Captain Seguín said,* "si cabalgamos
ahorita, tal vez encontraremos a su tío antes de
oscurecer." *"Miss Barrington," Captain Seguín said, "if we
ride out now, perhaps we'll find your uncle before dark."*

CHAPTER 15

Yo los acompañaré al campo y luego atenderé al
prisionero. *I will escort you and Nick back to the camp and
then attend to the prisoner.*

CHAPTER 16

Buena suerte, Nicholas. Que bueno que encontraste a
tus amigos. *Good luck, Nicholas. It's good that you found your
friends.*

ACKNOWLEDGMENTS

钅钌

Texas in 1836 was unpredictable. People's lives sometimes intertwined in unexpected ways. With respect
for the past, I tried to carefully place my characters beside
those who actually made history. It has been an honor to
include Hannah, Nick, and Jackie in the Battle of San
Jacinto.

Many thanks go out to Judith Keeling, Editor-in-
Chief at Texas Tech University Press; Dr. Jan Seale,
author and educator; Dr. Alwyn Barr, Texas Tech University; Dr. Richard Bruce Winders, Alamo Curator;
Katherine Dennis and Karen Medlin, Managing Editors
at Texas Tech University Press; Jerry Bloomer, Public
Relations and Secretary of the Board, R. W. Norton Art

Gallery, Shreveport; Tony Cuate, my encouraging husband; as well as the other readers.

Thanks also to all the staff at Texas Tech University Press for the amazing job they do.

And one last special thanks to Carolina Alvarez for her expertise in Spanish.

ABOUT THE AUTHOR

Treviño's Photography

Melodie A. Cuate teaches fourth grade gifted and talent-ed students. Her enthusiasm for Texas history as well as teaching inspired her to write *Journey to the Alamo* and *Journey to San Jacinto.* She is currently working on *Journey to Gonzales,* the next book in the Mr. Barrington's Mysterious Trunk series. Her short story *Mañana* is included in the book *Out of the Valley, a Mestizo of Genres.* She lives with her husband, Tony, in McAllen, Texas. They have a daughter, Erica.

ABOUT THE SERIES

Thanks to the peculiar Mr. Barrington and his mysterious trunk of historical artifacts, seventh-grader Hannah Taylor, her older brother Nick, and her best friend Jackie Montalvo find themselves transported from the social studies classroom to major events in Texas history.

ALSO IN THE SERIES

Journey to the Alamo